CCCCXXV
THE THINGS
WHICH BELONG—

THE THINGS
WHICH BELONG—

By

CONSTANCE HOLME

The World's Classics

'*The things which belong unto thy peace*'

OXFORD UNIVERSITY PRESS
LONDON : HUMPHREY MILFORD

' *The things which belong—*' *was first published in 1925. It was first included in* ' *The World's Classics*' *in 1934.*

CONTENTS

PROLOGUE

HE dropped the pen. . . . More strictly speaking, it fell as if weighted from his fingers. He had an extraordinary feeling that he would never use a pen again.

A flush came into Mattie's face, but she said nothing. He had always expected that, if ever this moment arrived,—impossible as it had seemed that it ever *should* arrive,—she would meet it with a flood of joyful speech; but now she was silent. It was the second time this evening that she had surprised him by her silence,—this wan and weary early-spring evening which marked the finish of a bleak and soulless day. Searching vaguely, however, among recollections which had left impression without form, he remembered that people often did fall silent at the late fulfilment of a long desire. . . .

Instead of speaking, she sighed. It was such a sigh, he thought, as the dying give just before they pass on into new life. In that last breath there is everything that they see before them, and everything that they leave behind. Mattie's sigh was like that.

Not that she looked like dying, as she got to her feet at last, heavily a little, but pushing her chair from her more quietly than usual, not in the almost rough way she used sometimes, as if the very furniture of the house clogged and held her ardent spirit. She stood beside him a moment, looking down at the letter he had just written, a splendid woman, growing old,—and older in the evenings than in the mornings,—but still full of vitality and fire. Again he expected her to break out into some form of expression, either of satisfaction or relief, but still she said nothing. Sometimes, as he knew, on occasions of this kind, relief took the form of a recapitulation of past miseries, and he would not have been surprised if Mattie had shown hers in that fashion. But dumbness seemed to have fallen upon her. Even her face had grown strangely inexpressive. There was no hint in it that she was thinking of either old sorrow or new joy. It was simply blank, as if it was no longer able to register the workings of the mind that lay behind it.

Turning away from him, she moved almost aimlessly across the kitchen. It was as if she had been switched suddenly on to another plane, and did not know any longer what to do on this. Stooping, she put out her hand for the poker, as if meaning to stir the fire, but she put it out to the wrong side. That seemed to paralyse her more than ever. She seemed incapable of reaching across to it where it stood in its accustomed place, but remained stooping, her hand dropped loosely at her side. It was only after a long pause that she straightened herself slowly, and, swinging round, stared about the room with eyes which hardly seemed to recognise it.

He continued to watch her, fascinated. It was all so *different*, he was saying to himself; not in the least what he had expected. If only she would speak! . . . It couldn't be that she was disappointed?—he found himself thinking, startled; and suddenly there came into his mind the absurd fear that, in giving her what she wanted, he had perhaps taken away from her something that she wanted more. . . .

She moved away from the hearth, and, as she did so, the firelight shot up, so that her shadow on the wall shot up, too, and became huge and menacing in the kitchen. Too big for the room, it·pressed itself against ceiling and walls, as if trying to force a way out of what was no longer able to contain it. He watched it struggle for a moment, saw it sink and leap in a still more furious effort, and then the fire dropped and it dropped with it. He waited for it to shoot up again, expecting every second to see it beat and battle afresh. But it did not shoot up again. Instead, there came presently into the stillness a little tinkling sound which showed that the fire had dropped still lower.

The window of the cottage had long since gone black, making a dark velvet background for the gold flower of the lamp at his elbow. The gardens outside were as blank as Mattie's face, gone out as completely as if it was only in the daytime that they had any concrete existence. The letter on the table looked a white, untouched square, with the impress of his handwriting barely visible upon it.

There was very little in the letter, but it had taken a long time to put it down. They had been so long over it, indeed, that already it was time for bed. The kitchen clock told them that, breaking the silence almost impertinently, and Mattie started. And then she, too, broke silence.

'Eh, well! So that's the end of that!' she said, from the stairfoot, speaking apparently not so much to him as to a hundred other things about her; and, turning determinedly towards the stairs without further comment, mounted them with her strong though heavy step, and vanished.

He sat still for some time after she had gone, feeling a little defrauded and more than a little exasperated. Even now, when she had spoken, her voice had told him nothing. It was rather unfair, he said to himself. . . . It seemed incredible that the great moment of her life should have come and gone, and that she should have had so few words,—and none too comprehensible words, either,—with which to greet it.

But she was glad,—he did not need telling that; so glad, perhaps, that only tears could really express her gladness. Probably she was crying upstairs, even now, weeping the tears which it is better not to stop. Because it was wiser to let her weep he stayed on where he was, watching the night deepen over the gardens and droop closer upon his cottage.

He was glad, too, he said to himself; relieved, too, even though he did not feel inclined to weep about it. He felt instead that lightness which comes with choice after a long and difficult approach to a parting of the ways. He told himself as he waited that he had hesitated until now only because he knew that the moment had not arrived. He had hesitated and rebelled, and therefore he had suffered; but he did not suffer now. On the contrary, in this curious, almost unbelievable way, he actually felt glad.

He got up, after a while, and on a sudden impulse went and opened the house door. He knew that the gardens were there, the moment he did that. It was only through the window that they seemed to have faded away. He could feel them stretching about him on either hand; could see, without knowing how he saw, the actual shapes of bed and tree. But to-night he felt no thrilling link with the place which had been in his charge for the last forty years. He had passed on, as Mattie had long ago passed on. He had written the letter, and he was glad.

Without being conscious that he had done so, he left the door still open when he went upstairs to bed.

PART I
HIS

I

T<small>HE</small> letter was still there when he came
down. . . .

He had known that it would be there, of
course,—had, indeed, lain awake half the night,
thinking about it,—but he was surprised to see
it, nevertheless. More and more, as he thought,
it had taken upon itself the quality of a dream;
so that, when he saw it again, a white shape set
upon an expanse of red-clothed kitchen table, it
met him with a shock.

He put it away from him, however, at once.
After that first glance, which was not so much
a glance as an actual physical encounter thrust
upon him as he came in, he did not look at it
again. But he was aware of it even while he
refused to recognise it. He ignored it, indeed,
with something of the self-conscious effort with
which one ignores a vivid human presence, going
about his tasks as if under actual human eyes.
That he was oppressed by it was evident from
the way in which he flung the window wide and
the door wider, as if in an attempt to get rid of
something which threatened to take up its per-
manent abode.

For this morning he was not quite so sure that
he was glad. . . .

Lighting the fire, he set the kettle to boil,
afterwards going into the shadowy little larder
to look for milk. His wife would be awake before
long, and he would take her up a cup of tea as
soon as the kettle permitted. Both he and Mattie
were getting on in years,—he seventy and she

sixty-nine—but they were able to do for themselves yet. It was a good thing, he said to himself, considering all that lay before them, that they were able to do for themselves yet. . . . He said it to himself more than once as he found a cup and saucer and the sugar that Mattie loved; passing about the house with the careless precision of practice, as well as with something more,—the delicate, kindly step of one accustomed to move in narrow and crowded places, and among fragile things like flowers.

And never once did he look at the letter.

The kettle was slow in boiling, for the fire burnt lazily, this morning. Fires were sensitive things, people said, which knew when those who lighted them were in trouble. . . . He checked himself guiltily when he found himself thinking that, because of course there was no trouble. On the contrary, there was a great deal of happiness ahead, as well as excitement and adventure and reunion and new life. The last especially appealed to him, because, as head gardener at Ings Hall, he was continually bringing new life into existence. It was surely always a wonderful thing to be about to greet new life!

Mattie would think it wonderful, at all events, in spite of her wordlessness last night. She had continued to keep silence even when he had joined her upstairs, and, as he had refrained from looking at her, in his delicate, sensitive way, he would never know now whether or not she had cried. But while he had lain awake she had slept peacefully,—peacefully, silently, graciously, —slept as he had hardly ever known her to sleep, for she was too active a woman, both in body and mind, to sleep very well. Indeed, for months before the letter came to be written, she had hardly slept at all. . . . But last night she had slept as those sleep who for years have felt themselves to be behind bars, until the time comes at last when they lie down with relaxed limbs and smooth brows, knowing themselves free.

It was a great thing, of course, to be free. Mattie had said it so often that he supposed it must be true. He supposed it, just as he supposed that he himself was not free, because she had said that so often, too. He had never been able really to understand what she meant, because he could not think of a freer life than one spent among trees and fruit and flowers. But she must know better than he did what freedom meant, because she had thought about it so much. Talked about it so much, too, year in and year out. . . . Yes, it was a great thing to be free.

The day coming in at the door was going to be a fine one, he saw, although he had known that, indeed, as soon as he opened his eyes. But it was a shrouded day as yet, with the mist still high above the river, and threaded in and out among the woods which surrounded the gardens. In any case, he could not have seen either the river or the Hall, for they were a hundred feet below, but even his usual glimpse of the fells across the valley, beautifully vignetted by the stems of larch and beech, was hidden from him by the mist.

It was very quiet in his special domain on its steep little hill,—very quiet and very shut-in. There were the walls around it, first, the big, mellow, kitchen-garden walls, and then there were the mist and the trees, and then there was more mist again. The men had not yet come to work, and there was not even the sound of an approaching footstep. The sun had not yet broken through, bringing with it that sense of movement which is largely the play of light and shade. Only the birds were awake and beginning the day in their usual rushing way; and the river, which never slept at all, but ran and talked all night.

It was quiet in the house, too, except for the lazy crackle of the idle fire, and the loud, determined strokes of the tactless clock. Mattie, he knew, must be still asleep, for if she had stirred he would have heard the bed creak in the room above. Even if she had not stirred he would have known if she was awake, for her vitality would have flowed down through the house and touched him as if with an actual hand.

He loved the quietness. He loved being shut in on the top of his hill, and would have been only the better pleased if there had been thirty barriers about him instead of three. This was the time when the place was wholly his, before his staff stirred in the bothy or climbed the hill from the park. The men, when they came, had an air of possession even in their tread, and in the way they handled things and struck spades into the soil. It was natural, of course, but he felt that it robbed him a little. He had to share the gardens with them. His employers had the possessive air, too, although not so much as the men, both because they knew their place better and because they did not strike tools into the

ground. But he had to share the gardens with
them, all the same. They said: 'What are you
going to grow just here, Kirkby?' Or: 'Don't
you think we might have so-and-so, this year,
instead of this-and-that?' So they robbed him,
too.

Not that he was one of those jealous gardeners
who grudge the stuff they grow even to the
people for whom they grow it. He was not
foolish about the gardens, or greedy in any way.
He grew things for a purpose, and he liked them
to fulfil that purpose. Only he *was* the gardens,
so to speak, after all these years, and when anything was taken from them it was part of him
that was taken away.

He was certainly *like* a garden, as he stood at
his house-door, looking out. When most people
open their doors and stare, the things outside
come awake, but they took no notice of Kirkby.
The gardens, as it were, did not even look up.
They were no more disturbed by his appearance
than by one of their own shadows lying under
the bushes, or by the long, ghostly lines of the
green and crystal hoar-frost.

He was old and gentle, like an English garden,
but he was hale, too, and not by any means
run to seed. His clothes, good clothes, now
pleasantly shabby, had a mellow tone which
blended softly with their setting. His fresh com-
plexion and faded but clear eyes had the pale
tints of some of his own blossoms. The very
droop of his shoulders was less like the slow curve
which comes with age than the gentle stoop of
a flower.

Especially he loved the quietness because it

was at this hour that he had a vision of the
gardens as he planned them for the year. This
was his creative time, these few moments before
the men came and broke and scattered his
thoughts. It was then that he saw the long
succession of colours and kinds with which the
gardens would sum up their rich total before
the winter came again. He would lose some of
it later, of course, owing to other people's follies
and fancies, and the stolid frustration of concrete facts. But some of it would persist, even
through worries and contradictions and the hard
blows of the northern weather; so that, by the
time the resting-months for the gardens came
round once more, he would always in some
measure have fulfilled his dream.

He was not always able to snatch these god-
like moments in which he controlled the future.
Often enough, Mattie was downstairs first, and
he could not call up his pictures while she was
working and talking. Husbands and wives were
so near to each other that they got in each other's
way over things like those,—things that had to
have you all to themselves, or they would not
come. But he always took his moments when he
could get them, because he needed them. His
days were poorer without them and the assurance they brought him, as days are poorer without a prayer.

And just now was the time when the vision
was strongest and clearest, when there was promise of new life all around, and still it was only
promise. Like all artists, he saw his creation best
when there was still nothing but a blank page in
front of him. It had then a clarity, a sweep, a

combined passion and restraint which it never achieved again after he had once begun to work upon it. It altered, no matter how he tried to preserve it. Alien ideas crept in, upsetting the balance of his scheme. Beautiful ideas they were, too, sometimes, but they were alien, nevertheless. Often he had tried to convince himself that the altered plan was all for the best; but, as soon as the springtime both of the gardens and of his inspiration came round again, he knew that the thing which he saw then was the finer and purer.

The whole panorama of the seasons passed in colour and shape before his inward eye, running at the same time through his brain like a well-known piece of music. Familiar as it was, however, it was also highly intricate, with its many different parts overlapping and intertwining. Not only was there the kitchen-garden to think of, but there were the glass-houses as well, fruit grown inside and out, tomatoes, orchids, carnations, violets. Then, down at the Hall, there were the rose-gardens and lawns, tennis-courts and flower-borders, and the long yew and beech-hedges to be kept trim and close. And besides all these there was the big rock-garden across the river, full of plants which, however much you might suppress them, grew as giants grow in a single night.

He saw the vegetables he would grow with the warm, homely thrill with which the farmer sees his crops, and the housewife her stores of linen and jam. The fruit he saw as an artist sees his finished task,—as gleaming jewels of price which you can hold and weigh in your hand. But the flowers he saw as the mystic and the dreamer see

Heaven,—not in concrete form, but as sheer colour and light, and an ecstasy of shaded tones.

He had, too, the knowledge which enabled him to see under the soil, as the geologist sees the strata under his feet, and the drainer sees where the streams run under the apparently dry surface. Beneath the quiet beds and the still grass he saw the forces of life already waking to work, sending the spring-urge through the seeds which had slept there during the winter, or conserving their energies for those which should be given into their charge later.

But for that insight and knowledge there would have seemed little enough encouragement from the brown waste lying before him, and curving away behind potting-sheds and glass to come back to him again along empty borders. The gardens were not actually empty, of course, for there were evergreen climbers and shrubs, patches of colour made by the remains of the winter greens, jasmine in flower, and the wing-like flashes of snowdrops and crocuses. But by comparison with his vision it was altogether desolate and barren, for in that he saw all the miracle of each season at once, smiled upon by a cloudless heaven.

First—and this he always saw first, and indeed it was already hard upon the heels of his vision —he saw the crimson *ribes* glowing over the countryside, that precious pink flame which appears so suddenly and amazingly among the pale yellows of the spring. Then—a quieter beauty, but equally as thrilling—the infinitely pure green that comes creeping over the brown thorn. He saw the purples of lilac and iris, the

cool white and green of lily-of-the-valley, the
vivid yet delicate spirit-stains of the azalea. He
saw red and white jewels hung by the thousand
on raspberry canes and currant bushes, and the
creamy ovals of new potatoes. He saw roses, not
singly, but in arches and flung handfuls, and
a cloud of sweet peas like pinioned butterflies.
Backing it all he saw green again, the young
live green of the early spring, and the deep, sap-
running green of the flush of summer. But above
all he saw blue, that colour so precious in a
northern county which is kept short of blue skies.
Lupins and forget-me-not and delphiniums and
periwinkle, and the blue that is never quite blue
of the hydrangea. When he looked across the
gardens it was chiefly blue that he saw,—blue
against the brown of the soil and the green of the
shrubs and the mist-wrapped sepia of the wet
tree-trunks.

Not every other gardener, he found, had the
passion for blue to anything like the extent that
he had. All of them grew blue flowers, of course,
filling their borders with them, and flinging them
profusely about their rockeries. But they did not
worship them, as he did,—did not wait and
watch for them, feeling, as they looked at them,
that what they looked at was pure spirit. Mostly
they preferred deep-coloured roses and rich
carnations, the tawny hues of chrysanthemums
or the flaming shades of rhododendrons and
dahlias. They did not seem to see the wistfulness
of blue against a northern landscape, and how
it was answered by the smoke-blue of far-off
mountains and the steel-blue of frozen tarns.

This year, however, they were to have a new

blue flower which had attracted quite a lot of attention at a northern show, last summer. It had been brought into being by a north-country horticulturist, and so naturally the northern papers had made a great to-do about it. One of them had said that the new 'dawnbell,' as it was called, had a certain quality which only a northern mind could have infused into it; and another said that it seemed to contain all the fundamental blues of the world, as the rose seemed to contain all the fundamental pinks. Kirkby had not quite understood what either of the papers was talking about, but it did not matter. All that he knew, as he paid his homage to the dawnbell in its airless tent, was that, set against the background of his fells at home, it would have the exquisiteness and the appeal of a little child.

But not only did he see the glory of the garden unrolled before him; he saw the daily work, the infinite pains which led to the production of it. He saw the trenching, the sowing, the thinning, the potting and pruning, the staking and tying, the watering and weeding. He saw the daily fight with the myriad living creatures which strive to share the results of man's labours with him. And, when he had finished with the growing, there was still the cropping, the gathering for the Hall, the London house, the shooting-box, the market. And when the heaviest work in that way was beginning to get over, there was the layering and manuring and dividing; and always the continual battle for order with the leaf-storms flung upon him by the autumn gales.

Not that he saw this side of his vision as mere

drudgery, or in any way secondary to the rest.
It was all one to him, indeed, and of equal
interest and beauty, for to the artist the craft is
as fascinating as the dream. *He* knew, who had
done every job in a garden in his time, the contentment that may wait upon a man when he is
working out even the smallest detail of a great
conception. Long ago he had learned that the
whole is implicit in the part; so that, while he
broke his way through stiff soil, or toiled
patiently with the knife, he felt his material
quiver with the message of all that was yet to
come, and saw, not the apparently trivial task
upon which he was engaged, but the beauty that
should be.

He was so still during the few minutes in which
his vision passed before him that the very bushes
and trees, chained and weighted with heavy
drops, seemed by comparison to be full of anima-
tion. It was as if the actual life were being
drained out of him in order to supply vitality
to the temporarily vivid picture. The light had
brightened a little, and the mist was lifting. Far
below, from the direction of the park, a sweet-
whistled snatch swam up to him through the
mist as the faint chimes of sunk church-bells are
said to swim up through the sea. The men were
coming to work. Behind him the kettle boiled
over with a sudden angry hiss, and at the same
moment he heard the bed creak in the room
above.

Turning, he saw the letter. . . .

II

ONCE again, however, he shut it out, firmly refusing to look at it as he stepped across to the kettle. Yet again his awareness of it was apparent in his every movement. His hand shook as he made the tea; and when the bed upstairs creaked again, with that sharp, emphatic creak which he had come to regard as actually emanating from his wife rather than as the mere protest of a piece of furniture, he hurried out of the room as if thankful to get away from it.

Cup in hand, he went upstairs, and entered the low bedroom, with its window looking out on to the little plot of ground which was private to the house, separated from the rest of the gardens by a privet hedge which he had planted forty years ago, and which had now grown thick and high. He had never ceased to feel surprised when he looked at that hedge, not because it had done so well, but because it was there at all. He would never have thought of planting it but for his wife, because it would never have occurred to him to feel the need of it. Either the whole place was his, or else none of it was,—that was how he looked at it. Nevertheless, he had planted the hedge to please her, because she wanted a spot where she could 'get away.' In the same way she had chosen the bedroom which looked out on that particular side, because it made her feel that she 'wasn't there.' He had had some difficulty in understanding either of these rather puzzling statements, but he had made no bones about them. He himself had never wanted either to get away or to feel that he wasn't there; but of course it wasn't to be expected that he and Mattie should always feel the same.

She was sitting up in bed when he went in, and leaning forward a little, as if some eagerness in her had sent her spirit before her to unburden itself to him. The paralysis which had seemed to afflict her on the previous night,—the result, perhaps, of over-emotion or fatigue—had completely dropped from her. This morning, indeed, she looked alive to her very finger-tips. Her strong, buxom figure looked hale and wholesome in its good longcloth nightgown. Her plaited hair, run through with silver, was still silky and thick. Her eyes were shining and her cheeks flushed. She took the cup from him in a grasp that was as firm and capable as when he had first known her.

'Eh, but I've slept sound!' she announced, yawning and smiling in a breath, while the vibrant tones of her voice, running through the room, seemed to stir up the atmosphere of the house, and even to assist at the awakening of the world outside. 'I don't know that I ever remember sleeping like that before.'

He nodded, looking at her affectionately as he stood beside the bed in one of those still attitudes of his which suggested the poise of a flower on a windless day.

'Yes. You've slept grand. You were tired, likely, with all that settling and such-like.'

She laughed at that, showing teeth that were still fine, and stirring her tea with a steady hand.

'Nay, not I!' she said in the same voice, the very strength of which was an added denial.

'It'd take a deal more than that to knock me out.' Then suddenly she sobered, staring thoughtfully at the cup before her. 'I was just sort of—satisfied—I suppose.'

He said: 'That's right! That'll be it,' in his quiet tones, nodding at her again, although this time she wasn't looking at him; the little action and the repeated phrase seeming to warn off something inside him that was making him feel guilty.

'I was dreaming a deal, although I was so sound . . .' She lifted her eyes to him once more in their shining eagerness. 'I dreamt I was There!'

He grew, if possible, a trifle more still. So far, he had evaded the letter successfully, but he could not evade this. In another minute, and in spite of himself, he, too, would be There. . . .

'I saw the whole spot as plain as plain!' Mattie went on rapidly. 'There was Luke's house, first of all, and then Joe's, and then Maggie's and her husband's,—all nearabouts together, just as they've always said.'

He murmured, 'Yes, yes! Yes, yes!' trying to hold himself back, but feeling that he was going, all the same.

'Ellen was there, too, though she lives a good bit off. . . .' She ruminated a little, as if trying to work out in her mind how Ellen had managed it. 'It was all just as they said, only a deal bigger. All of 'em together, just as they used to be, and things as snug as snug!'

'Yes, yes! Yes, yes!'

She paused a moment, contentedly sipping her tea, and staring at the knitted quilt on the bed as though she saw the whole pattern of her dream laid out there before her.

'There was another house as well,' she said presently, still staring,—'a house you and me know of, as isn't built yet, but will be, before long. . . .'

'Yes, yes! Yes, yes!'

'And between the houses there was that garden they talk so much about,—a great big stretch of a place as seemed to go on for ever and ever.'

He did not say anything to that, for the simple reason that he was no longer present to say it. He was There now, just as she had been There, all during those night-hours when he had lain awake and she had slept so sweetly. The garden had taken him, as he had known it would take him, if she began to speak of it. He could fight against all the rest,—the houses and their occupants, even that other house which was going to be so important, although it was not yet even built; but he could not fight the garden. The very mention of it was sufficient to drag him out of the safe place in which he had lived so long, and to carry him overseas.

'It was all just as we thought,' Mattie was saying again,—'only a deal bigger.' She had forgotten her tea, for the time being, and her gaze at the quilt seemed not so much to be seeing pictures upon it as to pierce through it and beyond. 'There was that much room,— more room than I'd ever thought there was in the whole world! Even the sky seemed bigger and higher than our sky over here.' She drew a deep breath, as if even in imagination it was a delight to fill her lungs under that higher and wider sky. . . . 'The children were there and all,' she went on, after a pause, her voice softening. 'You'll hardly believe it, but I knew 'em as well as well, even though I've never seen no more of 'em than just their photos! There was Luke's Joe, and Joe's Luke, and little Sally, and Daisy May; little Eric, too . . . and Maggie's last, as hasn't done as well as it should. . . . I couldn't have known them better if I'd brought them up myself! And the queerest thing of all was that they knew *me!* . . . Just before I woke up I told 'em I'd got to go, and they set to and cried fit to break their hearts.'

'It was only a dream,' he tried to console her, speaking with an effort as if from a great distance.

'Yes, but it wasn't like dreaming; it was like *being!*' she said quickly, and suddenly her eyes filled with tears. 'It was *that* real!'

He came back then from his leap across the ocean, and, reaching out his hand, patted her on the shoulder.

'It'll be real enough soon,' he reminded her gently. 'It's only a matter of being patient a few weeks more.'

'Only a few weeks, that's all,' she repeated after him in a curiously childlike fashion, heartening herself both with the words and with a sip of the cooling tea. 'But it's a long while, all the same. . . . Seems strange, doesn't it, you should feel as if you couldn't wait a few more weeks, when you've waited for years and years?'

'You won't notice you're waiting,' he pointed out. 'You'll be too busy. There'll be a deal to do.'

She brightened at that, her vitality mounting at the very thought of the approaching period of activity. 'Ay, and I'm keen to be at it!' she retorted briskly. 'I shan't feel it's really real until I begin to pack!'

She was launched now upon a subject of which the possibilities were endless, and was already deep in its details when the same whistled snatch reached them which Kirkby had heard earlier from the park. He moved automatically. 'There's the men. I must be off,' he said, turning towards the door.

Mattie nodded, her mind still full of delightful problems.

'It's time we were both moving,' she agreed, though vaguely. 'I'm late, this morning. . . . It's that dream, I suppose,' she added, passing her hand over her eyes as if to remove something which still lingered before them, 'but I don't rightly feel as if I was back!'

'Oh, you're back, right enough!' he smiled at her from the door; and at the words the thing which had stayed in front of her eyes fled, and she looked across at him.

'Ay, I'm back,' she said in a curious tone, and looked away from him and about her. 'Back!'— and her glance went to the privet hedge beyond the window. . . . He waited a moment, staring at her uncertainly and rather uncomfortably, and then slipped quietly from the room. Halfway down the stairs, he heard her say 'Back!' again, and hesitated in his step as if meaning to return to her; only to hurry on afterwards more rapidly than ever.

III

As he entered the kitchen he was met by the letter with the now familiar shock, but this time he did not attempt to evade it. On the contrary, he went deliberately across to it, and stood by the table, looking at it. A glance at the clock had shown him that he was earlier than he had imagined, and he was in no mood to meet his staff before he was obliged. That whistling first-comer would be Len Machell, a skilled gardener and his right-hand man. Len was always early, and he had always liked him for it; but he was not so sure that he liked him for it, this morning. Deep down in his mind lurked an uncomfortable suspicion that Len had a reason for coming early to-day. . . .

The letter, addressed in his small but flowing handwriting, was directed to his employer at the Hall. He was always slightly ashamed of his pale, delicate script, especially when he happened to see it beside his wife's black and sturdy hand. The scant imprint of the one seemed almost a purposed reproach to the brave intensity of the other. It was true that Mattie, in helping to draft the letter, had used so much of the ink, writing and re-writing, and underlining and exclaiming, that there had been very little of it left by the time he came to it; but of course that was no excuse. *She* would have got her effect, he knew, even with a dried-up bottle and a broken nib! . . . He felt unhappily that his effort looked even feebler this morning than it had done last night, as if it had faded for lack of volition on the part of the writer.

Yet, after all, he said to himself, straightening himself as he stood, it was his weak pen which had altered their destinies. Mattie's handwriting, superior though it was, could not in this case have had the weight of his. The ink that was left had been more than sufficient for the few, colourless words in which, after forty years' service, he had sent in his notice.

It had seemed so impossible a thing before it was done, and, now that it *was* done, it seemed so easy. Simple and easy, as death seemed, when you saw it close. . . . But it was wrong of him to keep on thinking of the change that was coming in terms of trouble or death. Once already that morning he had had to remind himself that what it really stood for was new life.

Yet it was only in terms of death, he said to himself obstinately, that he could think of the actual break. It seemed absurd that the snapping of a tie like that could be brought about by the mere scraping of a rusty pen. It should be accomplished, he thought, in some more dramatic way, like the call to attention of clean shot, and the lowering of something into a grave.

Forty years' service was in that letter, but there was so much more besides. He had been bred on the estate, like his parents before him, and he had never left it. All that was in it, too. Old customs and ways of thought, closer and closer growth to human beings and to the soil,— links that had loosened and even broken, but had always welded again,—all these were there. Not in the actual wording of the letter, of course, but in its very texture; so that it seemed as if one man alone could never carry its weight of association and memory, and its long tale of the years.

And more besides. . . . Not only was there forty years' service in the letter, but there was forty years' struggle . . . all that long contest between himself and his wife, which had begun in the first year of their marriage and never stopped,—never, that is, until last night with the writing of the letter, when it had stopped as a clock stops in a house where somebody dies.

Even this morning he had that same feeling as of a clock stopped somewhere in the house, followed as it always was by a silence that could be heard. . . .

Well, it was all over,—the talks, the disputes, the discussions as to ways and means. She had always wanted to go, and he had never been able to go; first, because he hadn't the money, and, second, because he hadn't the heart. He had grown to believe that the discussions would go on for ever, and now they were at an end. It almost seemed as if they would have nothing to talk about any more.

She had never liked the place from the very start; never settled or learned to look upon it as home. He had waited for the years to work their magic upon her, and they had never worked it. She had never settled. . . . Always she had gone on longing and reaching out for something that wasn't there, something that in the very nature of things couldn't possibly be there.

It had taken him a long time to understand, and he was not sure that he understood, even yet. All that he had definitely learned from the clash of wills was that the heart must face its own way; that one man's meat may be another man's poison, and that the holy, inhabited place wherein one soul can find its peace may be nothing but an airless vacuum to another.

Yet it was not, he sometimes argued with himself, as if he had taken her from such a very different existence. She was a gardener's daughter, as he was a gardener's son, and had been born to the same tranquil round and lovely isolation. He had thought her happy enough when he saw her at home, cheerful and busy and making her own interests; but that, as he knew now, was merely because of her youth. The soul can lay out its own pleasure-grounds when it is young. Later, when it ceases to do so, it sees the little ring-fence surrounding it only too plainly.

Right up to the time of her wedding, indeed, Mattie had been so busy, one way and another, that she had never realised her own requirements. Even if she had thought about them, she would have taken it for granted that marriage would mean a wider life, and, instead, she had found life narrow down upon her. Existence in her native place had been narrow, too, as she was ready to admit, but not *so* narrow; for in the home of one's youth there is always a way of escape through the magic door of childhood.

It was tragic that she had not known that she needed a wider scope,—tragic for both of them. But she had not known, and there had been nobody—apparently—to tell her. It was the

gardens which told her eventually,—his dear,
charmed circle of the gardens,—when it was
too late.

He had found her, one evening,—as very soon
after their marriage he had come to look for
her,—sitting beside an upstairs window. The
window was open, and by putting out her head
she could see between the trunks of the trees to
the coloured canvases of the fells. It was a cir-
cumscribed view at the best, with only a section
of the hills visible when the weather permitted,
together with a strip of sky laid nun-wise across
their foreheads; but it was better than nothing.
He had called up to her laughingly to ask her
'what she was at,' and she had told him in reply
that she was 'shoving the walls away.'

'Shoving what walls? And whatever for?' he
had enquired, puzzled, and she had flung out
her hands with a thrusting movement towards
the walls surrounding the gardens.

'*Them* walls!' she had said vehemently. 'They
make me feel sort of choked. There's times I feel
I could hag 'em down with my own hands, brick
by brick!'

He had been so surprised by that that he had
stayed under the window, staring, and wondering whether she wasn't well, or whether something had happened to upset her. It seemed
incredible to him that people should think of
garden walls as shutting them in, when everybody knew that what they were really there for
was to shut things and people out.

'What, there was walls at home, wasn't there?'
he reminded her, at last. 'Ay, and a deal higher
than ours, too, now I come to think of it!'

It had been her turn to stare, then, turning the problem over in her mind.

'I never thought of 'em as high,' she returned slowly, pondering. 'Anyway, I never felt shut in. Likely it was just because things seem that much bigger and wider to a child, but I remember thinking the garden was nearabouts as big as the whole world!'

'Well, I'm not saying this here's quite as big as that!' he had tried to laugh her out of her brooding. 'But it's a fairish size. You'll not find a better kitchen-spot anywhere in the North.'

'It's terribly shut-in, all the same,' she persisted obstinately. 'And terribly small. *That* small,' she added suddenly, with a characteristic flash which might have stood equally for bitterness or humour, 'I could happen put it inside my wedding-ring!'

It had grown no bigger for her, either, as time went on. She had never ceased to find it small and shut-in, never ceased to rebel against its limitations. Many a day she had sat by the upstairs window during the years that followed, but she had never succeeded in pushing the walls away. It was he who had done it in the end by writing the letter, laying them flat with his pen as effectively as with any Jericho trumpet.

Still, it was her will that ran behind the pen, even though it was his hand that held it. He knew that well enough, even while his loyalty had no intention of admitting it. The disputes and discussions had seemed futile enough at the time, but they had done their work in the end. Her hours of silent revolt, equally with her passionate clamourings to be free, had accumulated at last into a dynamic force which seemed able to move mountains.

Once, before, indeed, she had almost succeeded in getting her way, only to find, just as she was on the point of turning into it, that it led to a dead end. The affair was so long ago now that he had practically forgotten it, but it came back to him, this morning. Contemplating it to-day, he was struck by one curious fact,—that what he had nearly done then seemed to him now far more incredible than what he had actually done, last night. The sudden reassertion of that distant point of view showed him how much he had altered since that date; how far he had travelled, although unknowingly, along the road to Mattie's desire.

It was at a local flower-show that the opportunity had come, tumbled from Heaven, as it seemed, in answer to Mattie's pleading. He had been present at the show in the capacity of judge, and a visiting landowner had taken a fancy to him. At the end of the afternoon, his new friend, without actually offering him the post, had yet managed to convey to him that his own head gardener's situation, which happened to be vacant at the moment, could be Kirkby's for the mere formality of asking.

He had forgotten the incident, as has been said, but at least he had no difficulty in remembering how his wife had taken the news. It had acted upon her like a charm; turning her, even at the mere prospect of escape, into a different creature, so that already she moved and spoke as if breathing a freer air. All evening they had debated the question, and had gone up to bed

resolved upon accepting the unspoken invitation.
He recalled Mattie's elation over their luck, her
gratitude to Providence, her almost childlike
happiness. Yet it was he who had slept, that
night, even under the sword of impending
change; while she, for all that her prayer was
about to be granted, had lain awake.

And in the morning the whole of her evening
dream had fallen to pieces. . . . She had come
downstairs silent and apathetic, dimmed as a
candle is dimmed by the coming of daylight.
She ignored any reference on his part to the decision of the night before, and, when he definitely
tried to reopen the subject, she pushed it away.
Later, when he insisted that the matter should
be settled, one way or the other, she told him
that she had given up all idea of leaving.

'It'd make no difference, even if we did go,'
she had said dully. 'I didn't see it, first thing,
but I do now. It'd be the same thing over again,
that's all, and happen worse.'

His heart had leaped in spite of him at the
unexpected reprieve, but he had tried to en-
courage her, nevertheless.

'What, it'll be a fresh spot, anyhow!' he reminded her bravely. 'That's something, surely?
Fresh folks and a fresh house, as well as a different sort of air, as'll likely suit you better.'

She shook her head.

'It'd only look fresh on the outside. It wouldn't
be fresh in any way as really mattered.'

'If it's the walls as is still bothering you,
they've no call to, as I've told you already. The
house at the new spot is outside the gardens
altogether. I asked Colonel Brangwyn special.'

But she refused to be heartened.

'It'd be the same thing over again,' was all she would say, repeating herself endlessly. 'Just exactly the same. You and me and the gardens, and me choking myself to death.'

'What is it you *do* want, d'you think?' he had asked her at last patiently, and she had shaken her head again, looking away from him almost shyly.

'Nay, I don't know. I'm daft, I suppose. It's just *room*. . . . Ay, well, it's no use talking about it any more. But you needn't apply for Colonel Brangwyn's.'

Much the same situation had recurred at intervals, later on, but it had always ended in the same way. Always she had drawn back again at the last moment. Always it had seemed to her that she had found the right road at last, only to realise that it led nowhere. Always she had seen in time that, no matter where she went, to this country-house or that, she would always have the little ring of an English garden round her.

Things had been better for her after the children began to come, but they had also been worse. The gardens had grown fuller for her, after their arrival, but they had grown no larger. Moreover, the increasing family had put a stop to any chance of retirement as well as to the occasionally-discussed project of 'setting up for ourselves.' Money had continually grown tighter. With each fresh child that appeared, they were forced to 'plough a furrow nearer the fence.'

Yet, if it was the children who in the first instance had closed the door to escape, it was the children who in the long run had thrown it open. One by one, as they grew up, they had all of them left the gardens. They had loved them,—all, perhaps, except Ellen,—just as they loved their parents; but they had left them, nevertheless. Something of their mother's longing for space must have entered into them at birth, making it impossible for them to remain. And not only had they found the gardens too small, but England itself, so that they had allowed Canada to swallow them up, as it swallowed so many.

It was not long, however, before they began to regret this wholesale snapping of ties. Not only did they get together as soon as possible on the other side, but, the moment they were on their feet, they wrote, urging their parents to join them. Sometimes it was Luke who wrote, and sometimes Joe; Maggie, sometimes, and sometimes Ellen. Later on, when they were all married, the boys' wives wrote, too, and the girls' husbands; and, later still, it was the grandchildren who, with their first handling of a pen, added their unsteady scrawls to the general petition.

It was really the grandchildren who had beaten him in the end. . . .

IV

ALL the same, a long time had elapsed before he had finally given in. He was middle-aged and over even when the letters first began to come, and he had not felt able to face the venture. Mattie was all agog for it, of course, seeing it as the chance for which she had waited all her life, but he refused to consider it. He had said 'no' so often, indeed, that it had seemed as if he could go on saying it for ever. But he had not gone on saying it for ever, or anything like it. Quite suddenly he had blotted out all those accumulated 'noes' with a single 'yes.'

Yet, perhaps, now that he came to think of it, it had not been as sudden as he imagined. It seemed to him now, looking back, that the 'noes' had had no significance at all; that, in point of fact, he had been defeated from the very start. Right from that first occasion upon which he had found his wife upstairs, pushing the walls away, he had known that he would go. . . .

Nevertheless, for ten years at least he had successfully resisted both Mattie's persuasions and the calls from over the sea. It seemed extraordinary to him now that he should have been able to hold out so long. But then it was not he himself that had been able to hold out, but something outside him,—something that would not break, that never *could* have broken, so he had firmly believed, until it had given way on the previous evening.

Still, it had not been an easy matter, keeping his ears and his heart shut, all those years. Not

only were there Mattie's arguments to contend
with, and of course the letters, but there was
a constant succession of photographs as well.
Snapshots of the party across the ocean were
always arriving,—pictures of his children, of
their wives and husbands, their homes, their
families. And besides all these there were photographs of the nursery garden which they ran
among them, and which they were rapidly turning into a big business. For in this one thing at
least they had remained true to type. Without
hesitation they had turned naturally and successfully to gardening.

At first he had felt little more for their far-off
efforts than the aloof if kindly contempt of the
finished workman for the crude beginner. He
was glad, of course, that the children had kept
to the old trade, but conditions were different
'out there,' and at first he found them difficult
to follow. As time went on, however, and the
photographs showed the garden to be increasing
in size and scope, his interest began to quicken.
He had it fixed in his mind now what they were
planting and when, and what they were growing
for the different markets. Presently he was even
trying some of their new-fangled ideas on his own
account, although he was careful not to say very
much about them. Thinking about that distant
garden while he worked in his own, he came at
last to that point where the mind passes so easily
between place and place that the body might
equally well be in either.

Mattie, of course, had reached that particular
state long since. Her dream of last night had
been only a vivid extension of it. Often, for

instance, she would talk of the grandchildren
as if they were no farther away than round the
corner. 'Little Joe's first day at school to-day,'
she would say, bending over her sewing. 'I hope
they got him off in good time.' Or—'Maggie's
May's not so grand with that cough of hers. I
must see about getting her a bottle of something
from the chemist's.'

He had done his best to conceal from her his
growing absorption in the Canadian enterprise,
but it was not long before she discovered it.
Dropping her talk of the grandchildren to some
extent, she concentrated upon the business, surprising him, times without number, by her intimate knowledge of it. She, who had never shown
even the faintest enthusiasm for his particular
job, seemed to know every seed that was sown
in that nursery across the Atlantic.

'Potatoes have done well for them, this year,'
she would inform him, glibly reeling off a list of
varieties. ' "Grand Elephant's" the best, though,
they say. I'd like to try 'em. That sort we had
ourselves wasn't worth the planting.'

'Main crop *was* "Grand Elephants",' he would
remind her mildly, but without arousing her to
any excitement.

'Eh, now! Fancy that!' she would answer, in
a tone of polite wonder. 'And I never knew! . . .
Likely it's the soil or something as makes the
difference. Anyhow, all I can say is I thought
'em right poor.'

For some time she had contented herself with
merely stimulating his increasing interest, but
after a while she came out into the open with
it as a weapon.

'You'd settle sharp enough, you'd see,' she was saying presently, when the eternal subject came cropping up again. 'It's the same job, when all's said. 'Tisn't as if you'd be going to something different.'

'It'd *be* different, though, in lots of ways,' he had replied firmly, much in the same hopeless but obstinate tone in which she had so often asserted that 'it would be just the same.' 'Come to that,' he had added with spirit, 'I wonder you're so keen on it yourself if it's not to be fresh, seeing you've always been so set against gardening and such-like?'

She had laughed without resentment at his mild attack, too much enchanted with her happy project to be stirred to anger.

'It'd be different in *my* way,' she admitted,— 'I give you that—but I don't know as it'd be that much different in yours. It'd be bigger— freer—nay, I can't explain! But sticking things into the ground and taking them out again seems to me much the same job all the world over.'

He had said nothing to that, partly because it did not seem worth while, but also because his mind instinctively retreated when she mentioned size. She liked to think of the Canadian garden as prairie-wide, a great, untrammelled stretch of a place under an arching sky,—but that view of it repelled him. The photographs, of course, had shown him something of what it was like, but he chose to ignore them. Hidden away in his imagination was his own impression of the place, as a time-mellowed, sheltered circle of anciently-tilled soil. . . .

It was perhaps because he had been dwelling

upon the garden in that particular guise that yesterday he had given in. Also, he had had an annoying day, spoilt by several of those tiresome little incidents able to take the glamour even out of the work which is nearest to one's heart. But it was chiefly the weather which had overset his mind, hard and clear as it was with that sinister hardness and clearness which scarifies the soul. It was the only weather that ever made him feel really old, stripping as it did the veils from his various shrines. He had gone indoors for his evening meal, feeling that his life, under its present conditions, had nothing further to offer him.

The mail was in, he found, as he sat down,— it had seemed to him, of late years, that the mail was always in,—and a letter from Canada was lying on the table. Mattie had opened it, apparently, and presumably read it, but she made no attempt to force it upon his notice. She neither mentioned it, indeed, nor even as much as pushed it towards him, and, perhaps because of this lack of coercion, he found himself eyeing it longingly. In his momentary state of depression it seemed to offer him the exact stimulant which he needed, and, after resisting the impulse for a short time, he reached out and drew it towards him.

The atmosphere changed around him almost as soon as he opened the letter. Canada leaped out of the pages at him as he read,—Canada, live and free, and with red blood rushing in its veins. It had always seemed to him a country where everybody was young, and to-day more than ever it seemed peopled with radiant youth.

The letter was full of vitality, of hope, of healthy happiness and success. He forgot his annoyances as he read, and his depression vanished. By the time he had finished the letter he, too, felt young, breathing the air of that land which seemed to know nothing of growing old. . . .

The garden was in the letter, too, needless to say; in fact, it might almost be said that it was more garden than letter. It was almost as if the writer had posted a piece of the actual soil. . . . Kirkby, holding it in his earth-sensitive hand, found it an amulet transporting him so far that he lost all sense of his present surroundings.

He looked up after a time to find his wife's gaze fixed upon him, and the teapot suspended in her hand. Apparently she had been about to speak, and then had been checked by a realisation of the importance of the moment. He stared at her as if he found some difficulty in focussing her, and she lowered the teapot slowly to the table. . . . He tapped the letter.

'Mattie,' he said. 'We'd likely best go. . . .'

It was really the garden which had beaten him in the end.

V

HE came back from re-tracing the slow trend which had led to the writing of the letter to find Machell staring at his open doorway from across the garden. From that distance, as he knew, the man could see nothing of what was happening inside; yet he bestirred himself sharply and moved away from the table. Len's attitude affected him unpleasantly, just as his coming early had done; so that, when he went out at last to join him and give him his orders for the day, he had an uncomfortable feeling that this morning he was an enemy rather than a friend.

The feeling passed, however, as soon as he came into contact with him. Len was apparently his usual genial self, with nothing more sinister at the back of his mind than the preparations for peas and potatoes. The rest of the men arrived presently, and the gardens fell into their usual routine. By the time the sun had broken through, Kirkby was again beginning to wonder whether the letter and all that it stood for had been anything more than a dream.

The very weather of yesterday, that soul-troubling weather which had helped so largely towards his decision, now seemed like a dream, too. Looking at the fresh yet quiet colouring of to-day, at outlines diamond-clear and yet soft as human breath, he found it impossible to re-imagine it. But that was the worst of weather, as he knew, even although at the same time it was the wonder of it. You were happy on the good days, feeling that they would go on for ever;

but, on the other hand, the bad days seemed as if they would go on for ever, too. And the bad days were very dangerous, because they were apt to make you lose heart. On the bad days, if you were not careful what you were doing, you might find yourself signing the whole of your life away. . . .

Yesterday had been a destructive day, so bitter and killing that it seemed as if this morning everything should have been withered; but, instead of being withered, things were pulsing with new vigour. Even where there was no life showing above the soil, life spoke to him from below. The air, vivifying yet soft, had that baptismal touch which comes only at one time of the year. And running all through Nature was the thrill which comes out of nowhere, like the Spirit, so that the quiet land seemed to heave and thrill like sunlit waves of sea.

It came to him now that, next year, when the thrill was in the air, he would be in Canada. It would be the same thrill, he told himself hurriedly, because Nature's magic was the same everywhere; and yet it would not be quite the same. On the soil where you had been born and bred there was always something more. Not only did you feel the thrill of the spring that was coming, but the thrill of the springs that were gone; so that, with each fresh spring on your native ground, the thrill deepened because of the past.

That thrill, at least, if he went to Canada, he would never feel again. . . .

He had been right about Machell, he discovered later. . . . He discovered it after breakfast,—a breakfast which seemed to him more like a meal in a railway station than anything else. Beyond removing a few things from the mantel-piece, and routing a few other things out of a cupboard, Mattie had not actually begun her preparations for packing, but she managed to give the impression, nevertheless. The ebb and flow of her talk, rising and falling as she passed between kitchen and larder, came to him like the signals of approaching or departing trains. . . . Finishing his meal more hurriedly than usual, he went out to find Len again standing staring at the cottage.

This time, however, Machell made no attempt at concealment. Instead, he came forward to meet his chief awkwardly but eagerly.

'Begging your pardon, sir,' he began hastily, as if unable to contain himself any longer, 'but there's something I'd like to ask you. It's all over the place you're giving up your job, and I thought happen you'd put in a word for me if I was to apply for it.'

For a moment or two after he had spoken Kirkby did not know how to answer. He should have been prepared for the shock, he knew, but the fact remained that he was not prepared for it. Absurd as it seemed, it had not yet occurred to him that this sort of thing would follow naturally upon his 'notice.' It would have come to him, of course, with the actual sending of the letter, but so far he had not progressed beyond the actual writing of it. His intuition had been trying to warn him, it was true, but he had not been able to grasp what it wished to tell him. But it was clear enough to him now why Len had seemed to him like a stranger who might possibly do him harm. . . .

'What makes you think I'm meaning to give up?' he enquired at last, evading the question, and shifting his gaze from the man's face to the greenhouse behind him.

Len wriggled uncomfortably.

'Nay, I don't know . . .' he began, looking down. 'But it's been all over the spot for a long while now. They've got it down at the village, too. Mrs. Kirkby's always talked a deal about leaving, you see,' he added, rather more confidently, 'and lately it's seemed to me you were leaning that way yourself.'

'How d'you mean—"leaning"?' Kirkby questioned him a second time, and Machell wriggled again.

'Well, sir, you haven't been like yourself for a bit now, if you'll excuse my saying so. Absent-minded and such-like, and not hearing when folks spoke. . . . And, begging your pardon again, sir,' he finished, with a nervous burst, 'but you're getting on. It's only in reason you should be thinking of retiring before so long. . . .'

He found himself presently on the further side of the greenhouse, without quite knowing how he had got there, or what he had said to Machell before he went. He felt pretty sure, however, that he must have promised him his support, for he could still see the smile on the man's face, though distorted by panes of glass. But he had got away quickly because he had not felt equal to smiling at him in return. Indeed, never in his life had he come so near to experiencing the emotion of positive hate.

He understood now that he had never known how much he had valued his position until he was on the point of losing it. He had done well at his job, of course, arriving early, and achieving a horticultural reputation, not only in his own immediate neighbourhood, but in a wider district. Visitors to the Hall treated him with deference, and consulted him as an authority. He was invited to lecture, to judge at flower-shows, to sit on the committees of various societies. He had also written pamphlets,—one, upon an Alpine plant which nobody else in England had been able to grow, but which grew quite simply and easily for Kirkby; merely, as far as one could make out, because he wished it to do so.

Successful, however, as he had been in his own little world, he had never allowed it to upset him. He had never been over-elated about his doings, or tried to create an impression. Indeed, he had hardly ever thought about himself at all. He had taken the rewards of life, when they came, as simply as he took the fact of the pollen in the ripened flower.

But he had grown used to the situation, all the same. He had grown to expect the deference and the recognition, without knowing that he expected them. They had ended by creating a special atmosphere of his own in which he moved and breathed as naturally as in the air around him.

That atmosphere would be one of the things which he would have to leave behind him when he went to Canada. He would be nobody,—out there. People might be kind to him, of course,

might even like him, but they would know
nothing about him. If they thought of him at
all, it would probably be only as somebody's
father, old-fashioned and rather a nuisance.
They would never know that he had done anything or been anything,—out there.

He felt ashamed of himself at first for caring so
much about the loss of a thing like that, but, as
he pondered the question further, he saw deeper.
It was not just conceit and vanity that made
people want recognition when they were old.
What they were looking for when they asked for
it was a definite confirmation of their personality,
—a vital necessity, without which they were apt
to wither away. They were like cut flowers, he
thought, once they had lost their special identity.
That was why so many lingered on in the place
where they had lived and worked, feeling that
they would die if they were taken away from it.
Even those who had been neither pleasant nor
useful in their lives received some sort of recognition in the place where they had lived. The new
folks whom you met when you were old often
seemed tacitly to deny that you had ever lived
at all. You fought against it, at first, but you
could do nothing about it. Presently, perhaps,
you even came to see yourself through their eyes
as a sort of ghost,—a ghost who would never
have any future, and who had never had any
past. . . .

And, along with your life, of course, they
denied your work,—that work which was part
of you and yet was so much bigger than you,
and which you had fondly imagined would still
live on in people's minds, even after you, who

mattered so much less than the work, were dead and crumbled away. . . .

One of the several garden-cats appeared at that moment around a corner of the greenhouse, and twined itself lovingly about his legs. He could see another inside the greenhouse, sitting on one of the stages, and still another sunning itself happily inside one of the frames. They were an old breed now, which had been in the gardens for years—so old, indeed, that he had ceased to distinguish between the generations. For the same reason, and because of their puzzling likeness to one another, they had no individual names, but were known collectively as The Cat.

They were an ugly breed, he supposed, although he admitted it grudgingly,—brindled, with the darker spots of the brindling appearing invariably in the wrong places,—but he liked to see them about. It gave him a sense of pleasure to watch the sun bringing out on their glossy sides the tawny hues which went so well with wood and soil. He had grown so accustomed to them, indeed, that a cat of any other description about the place would have offended his artistic eye.

The Cat was another of the things which he would have to leave behind him when he went to Canada,—the things which already he was beginning to count over and to weigh before the time came to let them go. He wondered for a moment or two whether it would be possible to take one of the breed with him, but came to the conclusion that it wouldn't do. Mattie might not like it; the people at the other end might not like it; and most certainly the cat wouldn't like it. No, it would never do.

He pulled himself together, after a while, and went off about his business, but the beauty of the young spring day was largely spoiled for him. He even shrank from it, now, flinching when it called to him, attracting his attention with scent and sigh in the fashion peculiar to the spring. Instead of soothing and heartening him, as it had always done before, it now seemed almost to attack him. He shrank from The Cat, too, especially from the sight of the sun touching it as it stalked across the gardens; and, going into his little office to examine his post which had just arrived, he shrank when he found catalogues and circulars addressed to 'The Head Gardener.'

But most of all he found himself shrinking when he had to approach any of his men, fearing to find some other of them with Len's petition ready upon his lips. As it happened, indeed, not one of them as much as hinted at his going, let alone applied for his post; but he continued to shrink from them, nevertheless. Self-conscious with his staff for almost the only time in his life, he felt that they talked about him when they saw him coming, and talked again when he went away.

He felt sure, at all events, that they knew what was happening or about to happen, together with the fact of Machell's application. Discreet as they might choose to be on their own account, they must at least be aware of that. He wondered how long the question of his retirement had been discussed among them, and how much time they had given him. It humiliated him to think that the struggle between himself and his wife should apparently be common knowledge. Perhaps they had even betted upon the contest, he said to himself, bitterly, backing first one and then the other? Or, perhaps, he added, with a cynicism which was very foreign to him, they, too, had known that he would be defeated, from the start? . . .

VI

THE impending change, he found, was already at work upon the house when he went in to his dinner. The whole place was upset. Cupboards and doors stood open; shelves had been stripped; while the contents of the parlour looked as though they had been having a waltzing competition. There was a large packing-case in the coal-hole, and another in the larder. Things which were usually upstairs had somehow managed to get down, while other things, which he had not seen for years, were strewn about the kitchen. The very atmosphere of the house seemed to have been shaken and churned,—to have been stirred up as violently as Mattie stirred her puddings. If he had felt at breakfast as though they were already at the station, he was now absolutely convinced that they were actually on the steamer.

Only in one instance, however, did he make any comment upon the upheaval. Mattie, as far as he could see, had moved almost every piece of furniture in the house; merely, it would appear, in order to prove that it was possible to move it. He ventured to point out that some time would have to elapse before they could even hold their sale, and she answered him rather curiously as they sat down to their meal.

'Nay, I know it looks rather silly to be moving the stuff so soon, but I'd a reason for doing it. We've got to settle what we're going to take, you'll think on, and what we're going to sell; and I thought the sooner I started in at the job,

the better. But I found when I came to think
about it that I couldn't *see* the things in any
spot but this! In fact, it wasn't till I'd started
pushing and pulling 'em about that I could do
anything with 'em at all!'

'You do get used to seeing things in the same
spot,' Kirkby said, feeling at the sight of the
'pushed and pulled' objects surrounding him
much as he would have felt before a bed of
uprooted flowers.

'You do that!' Mattie agreed, passing a hand
over her heated face. '*That* used, you forget
what they're like altogether. Why, I found I
didn't even know the shapes and sizes of things
when I came to look at them!'

'They get part of a place,—that's what it is,'
Kirkby said. 'You don't see them as if they were
by themselves, but as if they were built in.'

'Ours seemed built in right enough, this morning, anyhow,—I know that! I never remember
them taking such a lot of managing before. It
was almost as if they knew what it was all about,
and didn't mean to budge if they could help it!'

It was warmer, this morning, Kirkby said, and
likely she was feeling it a bit,—looking out as he
spoke at the thin, young spring-glow lying over
the gardens, and wondering again how yesterday
could have been so different.

'Nay, it wasn't that altogether, though I'm
not saying it mightn't have something to do with
it. . . .' Getting up, Mattie set an open tart, light
as an autumn leaf, on the table between them.
'But I can tell you I was real taken aback when
I found I didn't even know my own furniture! I
made sure, for instance, as that dresser of ours

would be first-class for the new house, but, now I've had a right good look at it, I doubt it's over-big. Then I thought as how that corner-cupboard we bought would do nicely for our pots, but as soon as I got it down I saw it was too small. It's a queer thing, it seems to me, when you're so far out with your own stuff! It's like living with folks that long you don't even know their faces.'

'They get part of you,' Kirkby said once more, as he had said about the house. 'Faces or furniture, it's the same thing. They get that much part of you, after a while, you don't rightly seem to notice them.'

Mattie looked about her at the disordered fittings with a mixture of affection and distaste, much as a mother might look at a host of unruly children. 'Ay, they do get part of you,' she agreed reluctantly. 'I never thought I should mind parting with anything in this house. I never liked the things, as you don't need telling, even though we bought 'em together; nay, nor the house, neither. But I found, when it came to it, that I wasn't over-keen on letting any of 'em go. It seemed sort of cruel, somehow, to go leaving them behind.'

'You'll not think twice about 'em,' he assured her, 'once they're out of the road. There's no need to go fretting yourself over a thing like that.'

'I'm not fretting myself, not I,—nor likely to be! . . .' She laughed across at him, her lips curving and her eyes shining. She had always been a woman of a fluid temperament, easily up and down, but of late years it had seemed

to him that she had grown a little dry. 'Dry'
seemed particularly the right word, he thought,
looking at her to-day, reminding him as she did
of a thirsty plant that was lifting its head in the
rain.

'I'd be likely to fret, wouldn't I, on a day like
this?' . . . She leaned towards him, laying her
arms on the table, and emanating so much sheer
radiance of spirit that it almost seemed as if there
were an actual halo round her. 'Why, I've been
rubbing my eyes half the morning thinking it
couldn't be true! That was why I was in such
a hurry to get things sorted out. It seemed as if
it helped to bring it all that much nearer.'

'It's near enough, as it is,' he answered, in
perfectly good faith, and then looked up guiltily,
startled by something in his tone which he had
not intended to be there. But she was too busy
thinking to notice it.

'You're right, there! In fact, it beats me how
we'll ever be ready if we're to get off, this spring.
Old folks like us can't afford to be kept waiting
about. . . . It won't be too soon for them Over
There, anyhow,—I know that!' She laughed
contentedly, looking past him over his shoulder
as if she saw welcoming hands reaching towards
her, and welcoming eyes turned her way.
'They'll be sending word, like enough, as we're
to go by flying-machine!'

'You've not got word written to them yet
we're meaning to come?' Kirkby asked. 'We
ought to let 'em know by the first mail.'

'Well, I've not got as far as putting pen to
paper, yet, if you mean that; but the letter's
written all right! What, I had it off as pat as

you like before ever I'd had my breakfast! . . .
Come to that,' she added, 'I've written that
letter many a time in my head during these last
ten years,—ay, and set it down as well, just to
liven myself with the sight of it! . . . In fact, I've
done it that often, it seems almost as if there'd
be no need to do it now.'

'If you go thinking about it like that, you'll
likely never get it done at all,' he warned her,
but she only smiled.

'There's no fear of that! I've never had a
bonnier job to do before, and I'll likely never
have as good again! . . . Every spring when it
came round I've prayed as this might happen,
and it's happened at last. It was always worse,
in the spring. You can stand a deal of things in
the winter when you're comfortable like, and
you've your own hearth-fire; but you want to
be stirring in the spring.'

He did his best to nod sympathisingly at the
wistfulness in her tone, but he could find no
answer to give her. He had never known what
it was to be afflicted by the fever of spring-
wandering. He had never wanted to leave his
gardens at any time, but especially not in the
spring. Leaving a garden before the spring-
sowing was finished would have seemed to him
like leaving a child before it was able to walk. . . .

It was true, of course, that last night he had
signed his gardens away, and that, too, in the
spring. But he had only signed them away in
exchange for another garden, and the work
would be well on its way before he went. It was
not restlessness but weariness which had forced
him to a reaching-out towards new life; not the

spring-fret but the overwhelming pressure of
years which was driving him overseas.

'I just can't believe we're really going!' he
discovered Mattie to be saying, when his mind
returned to her. 'It don't seem possible. To
think we're going to see the lads once more, and
hear 'em speak! They'll have altered a deal,
I reckon, especially Joe. I always said Joe would
make something to look at, if he once got going,
and it's queer if he hasn't, out there. They say
the air's that grand, it's like fine wine. I don't
know much about wine, but I've always hankered after the sort of air that sounded like it.
I've sometimes thought I could breathe a bit of
it, after reading the letters. . . . Then there's
the girls, too,—I fair ache to set eyes on 'em.
Maggie, now,—she was always a good sort; but
I don't know how I'll contain myself when I see
Ellen. I thought a deal of 'em all, as you know,
and lads is always lads, but I've sometimes
thought I kept the softest spot of all for my little
Ellen!'

He heard the words at first as one hears a
familiar tune played from afar off, familiar but
unmeaning; but presently the intensity of her
feeling got home to him, and his outlook brightened. He had been troubled when he first came
into the house, jarred both by its chaotic state
and by the events of the morning, but as the meal
proceeded he found himself calming gradually.
It was impossible, in any case, not to find something infectious in Mattie's attitude; to feel, if
only as a pale reflection, something of her
ecstasy. With a deliberate effort he adjusted his
angle of mind, setting aside his preoccupation

with the things that he must lose, and forcing himself to turn his attention to the things that he would gain.

'They'll be taken aback, Over There, when they hear we're coming!' he contributed presently, more cheerfully. 'I doubt they won't credit it, at first, we've been so long about it!'

'Nay, they'll credit it all right!' Mattie laughed contentedly. 'Many's the time Maggie's told me she's dreamt we were on the road. All the same, they'll be on pins till we've actually arrived. They'll be thinking every day as we might go and change our minds.'

He shook his head without looking at her.

'Nay, we'll not do that. It's too big a thing, is this, to go playing about with.'

'Too big a thing, and too short of time. It's got to be yes or no with folks when they get to our time of life. Just yes or no. . . . Anyway, they'll know it won't be *me* as'll be likely to change,' she added, with a touch of defiance. 'It's you they'll be afraid of, if it's anybody.'

'They've no call to be afraid, nor you, neither. I've passed my word, and I'm going to keep it. I shouldn't have written that letter if I hadn't meant it.'

'There's many a letter gets written as is never sent,' Mattie said, half-mischievously; dallying, as human nature loves to do, on the very threshold of happiness. 'I was saying something of the sort only just now.'

'This here'll get sent right enough, don't you fear. . . .' He straightened himself a little, and his mouth set firmly. 'Where's it got to, by the way? I'll be making the round of the place, this afternoon, and I could leave it as I pass.'

She nodded a trifle vaguely in the direction of one of the cupboards.

'I sided it away, so it wouldn't get lost. . . . I could likely run down with it for you if you're busy?'

He said 'no' to that, however, speaking with the same air of determination which sat so strangely upon him. It might be Mattie who, in the long run, had brought about the present position, but dignity demanded that at least he should hand in his own notice.

'I'd best see to it myself,' he told her, getting up from the table. 'Mind and give it me before I go.'

'Likely I'd forget to give it you, isn't it?' she laughed; and then, still laughing, shivered. . . . 'It fair gives me the creeps to think how, if that letter never went, things'd be just the same as before!'

'They wouldn't be quite the same, no matter what happened. Folks pass on, somehow. Even *trying* to do things makes a difference.'

'A deal o' difference it'd make to me, I'm sure,' Mattie answered him cynically, 'if I found myself still landed in this one-eyed spot! . . . Ay, well, I won't go fretting about things, just wh⸲ they're shaping so nicely,' she corrected herself quickly. 'Anyway, I'm glad you've seen your way to facing the job at last.'

There was a hint of interrogation in her tone as to how he had arrived at his decision, together with another and fainter one as to how he was taking it. Standing, he looked away from her through the window while he answered her unspoken questions.

'It just came over me, as it were, that I might never see the lads again if I didn't do something about it. You go on thinking there's time enough and to spare, and then all of a sudden there comes a day when you think there's no time. That was how it was, yesterday. I just sort of felt I'd be rare and glad to see 'em all again.'

The tears came into Mattie's eyes.

'You'll never know *how* glad till you *do* see 'em!' she said, with a break in her voice. 'There's nothing like your own flesh and blood, when all's said and done. And there's the grandchildren an' all.'

'Ay, and the garden. . . .' He turned to her then, smiling a little shyly, a little shamefacedly. 'I've never let on to you about it, Mattie, but I've been fair wild to see that garden!'

She laughed back at him and his hesitation, triumph and good-humoured affection mingled on her countenance.

'You'd no need to let on. . . . It was plain enough, I'm sure! I've known for a long while now you were thinking a deal about it.'

'Ay, well, it'd be queer if you hadn't, I suppose,—you're that sharp! But I've often thought I'd like to take a look in and see how the lads were framing.'

'You'll be seeing how all right before you're a couple of months older! . . .' She got to her feet, too, and began sweeping the pots together in a series of joyous movements. 'Eh, but I hardly know how to hold myself in about it!

I was fair tongue-tied, last night, when you said
as we'd best go, but I'm that full of it all to-day,
I can't keep it from wagging! What, I've been
clacking to the furniture all morning for want of
anything better,—telling it all about it as if it
was human beings! You'd have laughed fit to
crack if you'd seen the way I went on. Len
Machell popped in for a word and catched me
doing it, and he looked scared out of his life!'

He stiffened a little at Machell's name, feeling
a cold wind blow in upon him and his manu-
factured enthusiasm. As before, the situation
had remained more or less in the air until Len
touched it; but, as soon as he laid a finger upon it,
it became concrete. . . . He said 'Machell?' after
her, not as a question, but as if weighing a sound
which, in the space of a morning, had grown
sinister and threatening. But she took no notice.

'I was making pretence this house was Over
There, and the furniture was the lasses and lads.
"Eh, Ellen, my girl," says I, hugging the grandfather clock, "I'm that glad to see you I could
cry!" . . . "And is this little Sally?" I says, kissing
yon little stool. "She's grown rarely since her
last photo!" Right daft I must have looked, and
no mistake, but I couldn't help it. I was that
chock with it all I had to get shot of it, one way
or another.'

She was laughing and crying as she talked,
busy living over again the absurd scene which
had yet been so vivid and poignant, but for once
she did not receive the kindly smile with which
he usually rewarded her attempts at humour.
Instead, he turned away from her again, almost
as if he had been wounded and wished to hide it.

'What was Len doing, hanging about the place?' he enquired, surprising her both by his words and by his faintly-sharp tone, for he was a lenient master with his men.

'Nay, what, he was only in the house half a minute or so! You've no call to be vexed with him, I'm sure. He just looked in to say you'd told him we were leaving, and to ask if there was anything he could do. He said his missis would be glad to come up any time to lend a hand with the packing, so I said the sooner we set about it, the better.'

'I never told him we were going,' Kirkby said, in the same almost angry tone, making her stare again. 'It was him as said it. . . . He said it was all over the spot, and had been for long; and he wanted to know if it was true.'

She answered him soothingly as she carried off the pots to be washed in the back kitchen.

'Ay, well, it doesn't matter, does it, one way or t'other? He'd have had to know, anyway, before so long. I must say I was a bit surprised to find you'd been so glib about it, but it makes no odds. He didn't tell *me* it was all over the spot, but I might have guessed it. Folks always seem to know what you're meaning to do a deal sooner than you do yourself!'

He picked up his hat from a side table, and moved towards the door. The impulse was strong in him to tell her of Machell's application, but he restrained it, being uncertain of her attitude. He was longing for sympathy on the subject, despising himself as he did for the bitterness in his heart, and knowing that sympathy would assuage it. But she had never seemed to value his position as head gardener,—had, indeed, constantly made him feel that it was something to be ashamed of,—and he dared not risk the reference. Yet he lingered before going out, still playing about the question, as if hoping that something or other might occur to ease the trouble in his mind.

'I can't say I'm best pleased to think Len's been settling our business for us,' he said, as she came back into the kitchen. 'He's paid to attend to his own job, and not to go prying into ours.'

'He hasn't settled it for us,—not he! We've settled it ourselves. And, as for a bit of gossip and such-like, I don't see how you're going to keep folks from taking an interest in those about them.'

'I don't look for Machell and the rest of the staff to go taking an interest in my private affairs.' He lifted his voice a little, and felt a flame rise in him as she laughed. This was the second time to-day that he had felt that sudden spurt of hate, and in his horror at its recurrence his bitterness deepened. He hastened to get outside the door in case the hate should suddenly decide to vent itself in angry words.

Mattie followed him to the threshold.

'It'd be queer if the whole place didn't know I'd wanted to go!' she said briskly. 'There's been times, I'm sure, when I've felt like telling it all round England. It isn't a crime, anyway,— not as far as I know. We'd a right to go, if we liked. As for Machell, he's a decent-enough lad. I don't see why you're so mad with him. Mrs. Machell's a good little soul, too, though she

hasn't much about her. Let 'em talk, if it pleases
'em! A deal o' difference it'll make to us what
they're saying and doing here, once you and me
are a thousand miles away!'

She stopped to draw breath both for fresh
laughter and fresh speech, and in the pause he
managed to break away from her. He went
slowly, it is true, still longing for the consolation
which he had been denied, and bowed by her
last words as though she had set a weight upon
him. The thousand miles of which she had
spoken were laid like lead about his neck. But
he went, all the same. . . . By the time she was
speaking again he had rounded the corner of the
greenhouse and was lost to her. He heard her
voice continuing for a moment, as if not even
the consciousness of his departure could force it
into silence, and then break as if something had
snapped it. He walked on blindly, not heeding
where he was going.

And neither of them had remembered the
letter.

VII

Hᴇ had intended to set off on his round as soon as he had finished his dinner, but in the end it was half-past two and after before he finally started out. Something seemed to detain him, whispering in his ear that this was the last time, and he could not bear that it should be the last time. It was not true, of course, since he would be certain to make the round of the gardens many times yet before he left, but he felt as if it was true. It *was* true, in point of fact, in so far as it was the last round of his period of settled service. In any case, he shrank and lingered a little before setting out, as a man shrinks and lingers a little before starting upon a world-circling journey from which he may never return.

Yet all the time he was longing to be gone, and to be able to ease the strain upon his nerves by fresh scenes and steady movement. He was still nervous of the men; the kitchen-garden still irked him; the sight of The Cat stealing softly across the soil still foolishly made him ache. But it was not until the gilded freshness of the short spring day began to dim a little that he roused himself to action, hurrying now where he had loitered and fretted, as if in a sudden panic lest he should be too late.

Passing the last of the greenhouses, he crossed between borders of box to an arch in the high wall, where there were cherry-trees nailed flat to left and right like the sticks of so many fans. There was a little wicket-gate beneath the arch, and as he laid his hand upon it he turned. Even from that distance he could discern the figure of Machell in one of the houses, and by the stillness of his attitude he could tell that he was watching him. Watching to see the last of him, he said to himself, bitterly! . . . Watching as he would watch him on that last day, when he saw him leave the home of his youth for ever.

Even when he had passed along to the right, so that the wall came between him and Len, he could still feel his eyes fixed upon him, following him. They troubled him, making him nervous and uncertain in his movements, conscious that his back was bent and his step not altogether steady. He became so obsessed by them, at last, that suddenly he swung round, certain that Len had followed him across the garden, and was watching from the gate. There was no one under the arch, however, and he moved on again, feeling hot and foolish; yet nevertheless the intolerable sensation of being spied upon remained.

Down the steep rush of the hill he went beneath tall, splendidly-spaced trees, the smooth grass between which would presently be coloured and starred by daffodils and wild white hyacinths. Under the leafless boughs of beech he could see the hills,—the mountain-land and moorland which ring in all this part of the country, except where, on the one side, it runs rolling to the sea. In the natural arches to his right were framed the long slopes of the park, and almost beneath his feet as he came down were the massed roofs of the Hall.

He had never thought very much about the Hall before, even though the greater part of his life had been spent in its vicinity. He had accepted it, of course, as the central fact of the situation, the reason for which he and his work existed at all; but he had not thought much about it. The gardens were his world, especially the kitchen-garden, and, once outside their limits, things were apt to seem a little blurred. There were many days when the Hall, empty and still, and wrapped in rain or mist, seemed almost as far away from him as his lads in Canada.

But to-day he looked at it as he came down, trying to see it, to take it in, so that, once safely photographed on his memory, it should never afterwards escape him. And at once he found, as Mattie had found with the furniture, that he could not see it. Instantly association was upon him, refusing to allow his mind to focus on shape or size. He could not decide whether the house were beautiful or ugly, dignified or insignificant, of this period or that. As he had said to Mattie of her household gear, it was no more possible to judge it than it was to judge a familiar face.

He had, it is true, an impression of fine stone, of moulded windows and doors, a wide court-yard, pillars, steps, and soft-coloured, slated roofs. But always he found it impossible to see it as it would have looked unclad and without its background. Always his eye went to the creepers which he had tended upon it, to the shelter of the woods behind it, the run of the park before it, to the long lawns and the gravel sweep and the curving boundary of the river. And even those he could not see as another person would have seen them, for he had looked at them so long that it was only the spirit he saw, and never the bodily forms which contained and expressed that spirit. . . .

Yet this place, grown so impalpable to him that he could not even focus it, had him closely welded to it. He knew vaguely that you could not separate him from it without hurting him, any more than you could strip the creepers from the walls without leaving a scar. House and land had grown impalpable to him because between him and them moved the pictures of his past, so that you could not sever him from them without damaging him, because what you would really be separating him from was his own life.

There was a centralising power about the mansion of a big estate of which those who had never been connected with one could have no knowledge. It was like a huge buoy to which you were attached,—so safely attached that, no matter what came or went on the ocean outside, you, at least, could never slip away. Those outside must often feel a little lost, he had sometimes thought, shrinking from that possible isolation even in his mind. But, anchored to a place like the Hall, you had no fear of getting lost. Although you could not see it because you knew it so well, it was at all events a background against which you could see yourself,—as small, indeed, and comparatively unimportant, but still more or less plainly. Once broken away from that background, however, and out in the open, —in Canada, for instance,—it seemed highly probable that you would not be able to see yourself at all.

He spoke to one or two of his men who were busy about the grounds, rolling the gravel or trimming the turf, but always with the same anxiety and suspicion which had afflicted him all the morning. They were not Machell, it was true, but each one of them seemed to him to represent Machell, and, when he left them, he felt that they followed him with Machell's searching eyes. . . . It seemed an incredible thing that he, who had always taken his fellow-beings so simply and so kindly, should now be unable to meet them with an open mind. It made him ashamed and angry, so that his glance refused to meet theirs, and his voice sharpened when he spoke to them, as it had done with Mattie during the scene in the cottage. Even the Hall servants he would have regarded doubtfully if he had chanced to come across them, feeling sure that they, too, knew what was about to happen to him, and would spring their knowledge upon him before he was ready to meet it.

But he saw nobody as he passed in front of the house, walking with what he felt to be a furtive step which he was yet unable to alter, and pausing only to inspect the rose-bushes fronting the long line of the low terrace. Nobody opened the door and came to him, or hailed him from the stone verandah. He glanced nervously at the windows over his shoulder, but nobody looked out. The whole place, indeed, had a strangely hushed appearance, almost as if it had veiled its eyes while this its servant went on his last round.

Hurrying in the same almost slinking fashion along the central walk, he came to the cliff-side, and stood looking across the beautiful, dangerous stream to the mountain-wall beyond. He could

scarcely remember a time when, passing through
the grounds, he had not paused just there, with
the great trees around and above him, and the
rocky river below. The wide view, passing over
the wooded cliff across, and rising by green and
russet slopes to that last long line of loveliness
above, sometimes many-coloured and strong,
and sometimes faint and phantasmal as a cloud,
had been all that he had ever wanted by way
of 'escape.' It seemed impossible now that,
yesterday, when he had needed it so much, he
should never even have thought of it. One look
at the open fells, at the swift river running black
between its carved banks, at the endless crossing
and recrossing of fine bough-traceries against
the colourless sky, and his sudden revolt against
his environment would have been as suddenly
stilled. Just that one look, and things would
have found their proper balance again; one look,
and he would never have dreamed of writing
the letter. . . .

He swung round on his heel when he remembered the letter, and stood staring towards the
Hall as if through its solid structure he could
see Mattie waving to him from the hill beyond.
Mattie would think that he had forgotten the
letter on purpose, and he did not want her to
think that. He could hardly believe that, having
spoken of it just as he was on the point of leaving
the house, he could yet have managed to come
away without it. He even searched his pockets,
as if feeling that, by sheer determination, he
could persuade it to materialise; stared at his
hands, as if thinking that they might contain it
without his knowledge. But it was obvious that

he had not got it, and with a curious incon-
sistency he felt furious and frustrated. He said
to himself that he wanted the matter over and
done with,—that he could not bear to have it
hanging on like this. He even retraced his steps
for a short distance, as if meaning to climb the
hill again in order to fetch the letter. If he had
discovered it in his possession at that particular
moment, he would have thrust it in at the Hall
not only with relief but with actual triumph.

But almost at once he turned again as though
somebody had tugged at his jacket. He was
tired, this afternoon, and knew that he would
regret the extra effort before he was half-way
up the hill. Time was getting on, too, and if he
lingered much longer it would be dusk before
he was back from across the river. And Machell
could take the letter. . . . He smiled a wry little
smile as he reflected with what keen delight
Machell would take the letter! . . .

He cast another glance at his view as he came
back, remembering how often he had tried to
persuade Mattie to find in it the release which
he found in it himself, and how dismally he had
failed. Mattie had had no use for it either as
a view or as an outlet. She had liked the space
and the height, but she had disliked the hills.
For her they had merely been other and greater
walls, which she could not push away. And she
had hated the river. . . . Besides, nearly the
whole of the view was to the north and east, and
Mattie had spent the greater part of her life with
her heart turned towards the west. . . .

Also she had not cared much for being seen
about the Hall grounds, even at those times when

the owners happened to be away. It was only
with difficulty that he had induced her to attend
any of the Hall functions,—the cottage-garden
show, the tenants' garden-party, or the servants'
ball,—and then she had appeared only under
protest. His employers had sensed the protest, he
felt sure. In as close and delicately-dovetailed
a corporation as that of an estate, it was always
easy to detect the person who deliberately stood
outside.

Nor had she ever attempted to make intimate
friends of any of the people in the district. They
would have accepted her all right, for she was
both amusing and clever, as well as a hard
worker. But, right from the first, she had either
rejected her neighbours' overtures, or accepted
them against her will, and gradually they had
come to acknowledge the situation, and to realise
that they could get no further.

He had spoken to her quite early upon the
subject, seeing where she was drifting, but he
had not succeeded in changing her mind.

'What's to do you won't take tea with Mrs.
Grisedale?' he had enquired one afternoon, as
he came in. 'I met her just now when I was
down at station after some weed-killer as hasn't
turned up, and she was right grieved about it.
They're having a few friends in, she says, for
that christening-party of theirs, and she's keen
for you to be there.'

'I just didn't fancy it, that's all,' Mattie had
said, although taking care not to meet his eye.
'It's a bit of a trial, I always think, talking to
folks as you don't know.'

'Well, that's easy mended, isn't it, and the

sooner you start in at it the better? Mrs. Grisedale, for one, 'll not take you long. She seems
a decent little soul.'

'Oh, ay, she'll do.'

'There's Mrs. Ellwood an' all,—she's asked
you time and again. She told me she'd never
taken to anybody as she's taken to you.'

'And she'll do, too.'

'Well, then, what's to do you can't make
friends with the pair of them?' Kirkby had
blundered on. 'You couldn't have a nicer couple
of folks than them two, and you'll be wanting
somebody.'

But he had had to probe for some time before
she would give him the explanation.

'It's like this,' she had said at last, half-
ashamed, as he could see, and yet determined
upon her line of action. 'It just isn't worth while.
Making friends takes a deal of time and a deal of
patience, and, once you've got 'em made, it takes
a deal of getting over if you've got to leave them.
Well, it isn't worth it. I'm set on getting away
from this spot, as you don't need telling, and, if
I take up with any of the folk, it'll all be wasted.'

'Nay, what, friendship and such-like is never
wasted, surely!' he had affirmed stoutly. 'I don't
hold with gardeners getting too thick with folks,
nor their wives, neither. There's some as'll seek
you out just for the sake of what's behind you.
But it isn't good, all the same, to be always by
yourself, and a few nice friends'd likely help you
to settle down.'

But, unfortunately for his cause, he had hit
on the one plea that was least likely to weigh
with her.

'Nay, but that's just what I don't want to do,' she had said, looking past him, with the effect, which he was later to know so well, of seeing beyond him into great distances. 'I don't know how to put it, but it would be wrong for me, would that. It'd be losing something as is right down necessary to me. If making friends with folks is going to mean settling down, then I'm best without it.'

That part of the explanation he had been quite unable to understand, so he had concentrated upon the other.

'I don't see there'll be that much wasted just by you going to Mrs. Grisedale's christening-party!' he had said humorously. 'It seems a real pity you shouldn't have a pill-gill now and then. I've always thought you were just cut out for going amongst folks and keeping 'em all lively.'

At all events he had succeeded in making her laugh at that; changing her, to his relief, from the far-gazing woman who chilled him with her strangeness to the brisk, cheerful girl whom he had sought in marriage.

'Ay, I generally manage to make a stir, wherever I am!' she had said gaily. 'I'm not one for sitting mum in corners, and never was. If I'd had luck to hit on a spot I liked, I'd have done as much as anybody to keep things going; but it's no use thinking about it here.'

And she had never swerved from her determination during the years that followed,—never swerved at heart, that is, for she had not been hard and fast about it. She had got to know both Mrs. Grisedale and Mrs. Ellwood, in the end, as well as the usual run of people in the

district. She had gone to parties in her time.
She was never behindhand, either, when help of
any sort was required, for she was a kind enough
woman, in spite of her discontent. But she had
never got to the point of making intimate friends.
Always she had looked beyond her neighbours
to that distant thing in which they had neither
lot nor part.

Descending the steep steps which led to the
water's edge, he came to the catamaran moored
in its pool between the wooded sides of the worn
gorge. Going aboard, he began to wind himself
from bank to bank, the light, wooden raft moving easily on its steel pulleys. The water was
quiet enough here, black and almost still, but on
either hand he could see the fretted rush of one
of the fastest streams in England. A beautiful
river, winding and sweeping and leaping. . . .
A river which could rise in a few hours and become a broad, flying torrent, with crisp, curling
waves like those of the neighbouring sea.

And at once, almost the very moment, it
seemed, that he pushed off, the ache at his heart
left him, succumbing to that curious influence
which water has upon the human mind. The
detachment it breeds worked upon him even
in that black pool which could for no more than
a moment give pause to the sea-going mountain
stream. The smooth rush out across the un-
rippled surface was a steady rush into peace.
His nerves eased in the gliding movement of the
raft, held to earth though it was by that velvet
pull on its under side. He drew deep breaths as
he worked at the creaking handle. His released
mind took to itself wings.

For he had been a boy on this river, and
nothing that life had so far attempted to give
him had ever equalled that. He had been a boy,
climbing among its rocks, swimming in its pools.
watching its hidden life and learning its hidden
lore. He had known it empty almost as a sand-
channel is empty when the water alters its
course; seen it foaming and full, a swirling engine
of destruction. It had been the playground of
his youth, and at the same time it had been his
friend, for to his young mind it had had all
the personality and importance of a dominant
human being.

He was a boy again now, as he grounded the
raft softly, and softly stepped off on the other
side, as if stepping into a church. Here, where
he had spent so many hours with other lads, or
alone, there lingered for him still the holy touch
of youth. It was in the water and in the air, in
the colour and shape of things, and in the
peculiar values of the light. Above all, it was
in that atmosphere of childhood which never
changes, and which is so distinct from any other
that it can be recognised even in the dark.

He stood for a moment or two after he had
landed, surrendering himself joyfully to the
ancient thrill, and seeking from point to point
for reminders which should serve to accentuate
it. Here, where a low bough, along which he
had often walked, still thrust out its bold and
crooked arm over the racing water. . . . There,
where the salmon rose in the summer . . . where
the bathing-strand lay firm and dry . . . where
the long curve of the rose-gardens against the
river even at this time of the year showed a velvet

line. It seemed to him as he stood, quivering to the thrill, that never until now had he grasped the meaning of its peculiar comfort. Its virtue lay in that easy leap back to childhood, which made of life such a little thing, and at the same time held such a vivid assurance of a life that should be eternal.

But you could never hope to receive that comfort except in the home of your youth. No other place would do; not Canada, nor another. . . . In any other place you would have to grow old patiently without that blessed assurance, and to bolster up your faith in a future existence as best you might.

He had planned to get face to face with the Canadian problem as soon as he was safely across the river, out of reach of the staring eyes of his staff and of Mattie's exultation. He had meant to set forth to himself the advantages of the change, to conjure up the presence of his children and to dwell happily upon the interest of their garden. He had meant to meet, once for all, the call of the things he would have to leave, so that, no matter what else might lie before him, he could never suffer as much again. He had intended to return from his round already passed over in spirit to the new life in the new country, having said good-bye once and for all to the life he had lived in the old.

But he found that he could not think of either his lasses or his lads as he climbed the shallow steps which guided him up the rock-garden, strive as he might to picture them in their far homes under that high sky of which Mattie had spoken so often and so fondly. They were not real to him on this ground where, the instant he set foot on it, he relinquished his own manhood. Always they slipped away from him as ghosts might slip away. He had, indeed, one rather frightening moment when he found that he could not even remember their names.

He wandered for a long time in his country of the past, including both past and present in his gesture of farewell. At point after point along the paths he stopped to dream and stare, seeing the long, plant-carpeted terraces which he had planned, and could not have told whether they were the old or the new things that he saw. But in any case it did not matter. The old and the new were fused for the time being to make a greater loveliness, a finer air; that special atmosphere in which he lived again his own enchanted youth, and was permeated, as he looked, by the happiness which is a foretaste of the happiness of eternity.

Some inward monitor brought him back again at last to the raft, set his fingers to the stiff handle, and pushed him off across the quiet water. The mist was high above the river by now, so that, as he passed into it, he was lost to sight from either bank, with only the melancholy creaking of the machinery to locate his whereabouts. But he did not feel lost, because of the coloured picture of youth which still glowed and moved upon the vaporous canvas before him. He was still at peace, still sure both of this world and the next, when he met the further bank with a sudden shock.

There came back to him with the shock the realisation not only of his physical but of his

mental position. Climbing up the wood-edged
steps, he rose both out of the mist and out of
the boyhood dream which had so contentedly
ensnared him. He looked back for a moment
before turning resolutely towards the Hall, and
saw the mist lying like a shroud, not only upon
the river, but upon the precious things of his
own past.

He had lingered and dallied during the last
hours as if time had suddenly ceased to be, so
that he was forced to hurry now in order to
make up for it. All day, he thought, he had
been behaving like that, alternately dawdling
and hurrying, and then forgetting and dawdling
again. . . . The men had disappeared who had
been working in the grounds, and were no doubt
up at the kitchen-garden, waiting for him. It
was pay-day, too, he remembered suddenly,
with quick dismay, and they would not be best
pleased at being kept waiting for their money.
They would say it was time he went, he told
himself, as he skirted the still-silent house, and
came again to the steep path which mounted
his own hill. They would echo the words which
Machell had all but spoken, that morning,—
that it was patent to all and sundry that he was
getting too old for his job.

He had no difficulty now in thinking of his
children over the sea, less than no difficulty in
remembering their names. The whole Canadian
project came back to him, with all that it en-
tailed, together with the memory of yesterday's
fatal promise. He could no longer hide from
himself that, for him, at least, that promise had
been fatal, whatever it might mean for Mattie.

It was a knife set at his own throat, a pair of shears at his own roots. Even if he had not known the truth before he started on his round, he could not have helped but know it after those hours across the river.

The men were waiting for him, as he expected, and he paid them hurriedly, taking care not to look at them, and without any of the little kindly enquiries and comments which he often had for them. He had hoped that Machell, being the first paid, would be the first to go, but, instead, he lingered behind the others. Coming out of his office, he found him waiting for him outside, looking rather unhappy.

'If you could spare me a minute, sir . . .' he began, looking more abashed than ever by Kirkby's movement of recoil. 'I just wanted to say I hope I didn't put you about by what I mentioned to you this morning.'

'Why should it put me about?' Kirkby asked, looking, not at him, but at The Cat, which, moving tawnily between the white purity of the evening light and the warm brown of the soil, had developed an unearthly beauty of its own.

'No reason at all, I'm sure, if you're really meaning going. But it struck me afterwards, thinking about it, that perhaps I'd been over-smart.'

'You've got to put in early, these days, if there's a job going begging,' Kirkby said, wishing so earnestly that the man would go that he felt as if he were pushing him.

'Yes, sir, I know. And there's others to think of, too. . . . But I should be sorry if I'd put you

about. It's seemed to me all day as you were
a bit down——'

But to be told that he looked 'down' was more
than Kirkby could bear,—more than he could
bear to know that he carried the mark of his
defeat. . . . Waving both Machell and his consolation away, he turned on his heel.

'You've no call to worry yourself, my lad,' he
found himself saying, both his sense of justice and
his native politeness forcing him to the speech.
'You get off home. If I do send in my notice,
you'll be more than welcome to the job.'

He heard Machell begin to speak again as
he walked away,—broken but grateful phrases,
ending bravely with: 'If you're stopping on,
there'll be nobody better pleased than me . . .'
followed presently by the sound of the man's
footsteps receding along the path. He turned
then, and watched him walk across the gardens,
noticing, as he thought, the already-possessive
glance which he cast on either hand. At the gate
Len stopped and looked back towards the elder
man, and even at that distance their glances
seemed to meet and mingle as over some prone
and coveted body. When finally he had closed
the gate and disappeared, there came from Kirkby's lips a little sound that was like a cry. . . .

It occurred to him presently that Mattie would
be waiting for him, as other people had already
waited, that day, and he turned mechanically
towards the house. He shrank, however, as he
remembered the state of the place as he had
found it, earlier on, as well as from the fresh
transports which Mattie would have in store for
him. He felt, as he had felt about Machell's

rough attempts at sympathy, that he could not bear them just now. . . . Swerving away to the right before he reached his home, he took a path which led him beyond the walls into the healing quiet of empty spaces.

The spring evening was very still, so still that, as he stood, he could hear the faint cry of new-born lambs from across the river. All over the land was that cool silver light which is so much more mystic, and at the same time more inti-mate, than any other. An incredible gentleness had come upon the earth under its touch. Bathed in that heavenly light it became suddenly more human. Beneath it, the brown plough lay warm and rich, while the grassland looked springy and deep, a comfort to eye and foot. The woods to the west showed silver palings between their trunks; while, down on the flat, the plantations looked like clumps of sepia feathers. In the soft yet clear air everything seemed to draw together, the white-faced farm-houses, the woods, the hills, the gentle, coloured earth . . . gathered to hear the happy message with which the whole world seemed to thrill.

High on a bough above him a blackbird began to sing, and again there came from Kirkby's lips that sound that was like a cry. . . .

In the drawn dusk he wandered about the gardens, seeing the glass-houses, which were so brisk and coloured in the day, ghostly as water is ghostly under the first finger of the dark. Mattie had made no attempt to look for him, so that he was alone, as he had been in the early hours, but without the solace of his vision. The procession of the year no longer marched in strength before him, sounding its coloured trumpets as it passed. When he came to the place where the dawnbell was to stand, he could no longer picture it blue and exquisite against the soil.

For the third time that day rage seized him as he stood looking down at the dark ground which had blossomed so easily for him in the morning, but from which he could now conjure nothing but despair and gloom. He knew definitely now that he had been trapped by fate, and felt none the less bitter because he had sprung the trap with his own hand. He thought of his children with love, but knew that for such as himself there were things which were more than children. Closer to him than breathing, and nearer than hands and feet. . . . His children had grown away from him and made a life for themselves; but he, if he was to follow them, could do nothing but pine and die.

He made up his mind as he stood that he would go back on his word, and that after to-day he would shut his ears to Mattie's pleadings for ever. If she must go, she must go alone, and he must manage as best he might. The letter had not been delivered yet, as far as he knew, and, even if it had, he could always withdraw his notice. They would not be hard on him at the Hall, knowing well enough as they did what had brought him to this pass. For, in writing that letter, he had been trapped . . . trapped! The rage in him was so great that he shook with it as he stood, clenching and unclenching his hands and grinding his teeth. This time he actually cried aloud, and it seemed to him that the cry rushed out and over the walls, so that even down at the Hall they could hear him shouting that he was trapped. . . .

And then suddenly Mattie's face came to him as he had seen it, that morning, fresh and sweet and glad after her dream-tryst of the night. He saw the light in her eyes, and heard the break in her voice. He thought of her years of beating against the bars, and of how, for her, the trap he had sprung for himself meant the opening of her prison-gate. Remembering these things, he knew that he could not break his promise. . . . Slowly his rage subsided and his hands un-clenched. He stood, an indistinct figure in the dusk, with drooped shoulders and bowed head. He had promised Mattie, and he could not fail her. Perhaps, once safely Over There, he might be allowed to find peace, and forget.

. . . . .

Turning towards the house, he saw Mattie running and stumbling towards him across the gardens.

PART II
HERS

I

MATTIE never forgot what she had felt when she awoke on that miracle-morning,—never forgot, and never allowed herself to remember. . . . She came back to consciousness still swathed and steeped in the sweetness of her dream; arriving presently, with a little shock of joy, at the thought of the sweeter fulfilment which was to follow. At the moment, however, she found it difficult to believe that the latter could possibly be more concrete than the former. So real, so intense had been that experience of the spirit, that the senses also seemed to have been satisfied by it for the time being.

She lay on for some time after she had told Kirkby of the beautiful journey that she had taken in the night, living it over again to fresh thrills of delight which were like little inward cries of pleasure. (*So* they had looked and spoken, and held, and kissed. . . .) It was not often, except in the case of illness, that she had allowed herself the luxury of staying in bed. Very occasionally she had yielded to it when life was pressing too hardly upon her, watching the hours drift by with a hopelessness which was in itself a sort of hope, knowing as she did that, when that phase was over, she would be able to take up existence again a little more cheerfully. But she had never yet stayed in bed because the moments in front of her were so rich and wonderful that she could afford to waste them. . . . A sort of radiance seemed to her to pervade the room, in which the earthly day had not yet quite prevailed, so that she felt that, if anybody should look in upon her, just then, they would see her through a wall of light.

She had said to Kirkby that she was 'back,'—back in her prison, she had meant,—speaking the word with a bitterness which had first driven him out, and then almost brought him back to comfort her; but he was barely out of the room before she was gone Canada-wards again. She had forgotten so much about Them, she said to herself, half-ashamed to have forgotten, and wholly enchanted by the reminder. She had forgotten Luke's habit of cocking his head on one side as he talked, and Joe's love of humming a tuneless tune, while he drummed out the beat of it on his knee. Maggie's shrug of the shoulders, and Ellen's trick of half-closing her eyes when she laughed, together with that little way she had of touching you affectionately when she sat beside you. . . . Joe's eldest boy hummed, too, and Ellen's baby shut its eyes in the same fascinating fashion. It put out its hands to you in the same way,—little, round, baby hands groping half-consciously for the comfort of human touch.

It was astonishing, she thought, that people who cared for their children should forget so much about them. Not, of course, that you forgot *them*. You had only to think of them,—sometimes it happened without your thinking,—and their faces came up before you, in a sort of halo of light. But the little tricks and ways which held so much of their character seemed to fade if you were parted from them for years. Perhaps it was as well that they should fade, seeing how much they could hurt you to remember.

It had not occurred to her that she might be going to dream about the children when she went upstairs to bed. Indeed, to be perfectly frank, she had hardly thought about them at all. A great exhaustion had fallen upon her as soon as she realised that her forty years' struggle against circumstances was over. It had been hard to realise it, too. Even while Kirkby was writing the letter, she had found it difficult to believe that he was really doing it. Each moment, also, she had expected that he would break off and refuse to finish, and had found it incredible that he should continue calmly to the end. Indeed, he had puzzled her, last night, as much as she had puzzled him. To her, too, as to him, it had seemed impossible that the mere writing of a letter could bring so much to a close.

Even when it lay before her, addressed and sealed, and Kirkby, without any sign of repentance, had let it lie, she had felt no sensation either of joy or triumph. Instead, she had felt that great weariness, as after a heavy burden at last laid down, together with a curious impression of being out in a great space, without any sense of direction. She had seen herself, during those few moments in which she groped aimlessly about the kitchen, as a coloured balloon, broken suddenly from its tether, and drifting out across the world at the light mercy of the winds.

Nor, when she was alone upstairs, had she felt any glow of happiness over her victory. She had not cried, as Kirkby, sitting and waiting below, had imagined her to be crying. She had simply undressed as rapidly as possible, still feeling that curious unsteadiness as she moved about the room; and, once in bed, had seemed to pass instantly to that far-off place which was still more real to her perceptions than anything that she saw around her.

She had not visualised herself as going, nor could she remember anything about her actual arrival. She had merely found herself There, already a settled member of the little community. But she had known well enough when the time came for coming away; perhaps because, after all those years of longing, it was easier to get There than to leave.

She had seen herself passing between the houses, moving from one to the other with the assurance of long custom, and never once feeling that anything was strange. She had known which paths to take, which windows to look through, which rooms to enter. She had known that you always had trouble with Maggie's doors, and that Ellen's water-supply wasn't as good as it might be. She had known that Luke had a piano, and that Joe (who hadn't risen to one yet, in spite of his fondness for humming), sent his children to Luke's to practise. She had known the hours they kept, the clothes they wore, their furniture and their meals, their neighbours and their hired men. And they had known that she knew. She had fitted into their midst as a glove fits a hand which has never taken it off.

And other things, too,—the sort which nobody told, and which couldn't by any chance have got into their letters. Just when Maggie's husband was a bit tiresome with Maggie, and where Joe's missis failed in being just what he had hoped she would be. . . . Those queer sisters-in-laws of

Ellen's; and Luke's father-in-law, who was the
sort you could quite well do without. . . . The
trouble about the bit of money which Joe had
lent Maggie's husband. . . . The trouble about
the bit of money which Ellen had lent Joe. . . .

It surprised her to remember how much at
home she had felt, how completely in tune with
conditions which she had never experienced in
the flesh. Why, she had even felt at home in the
house which she had seen as already built for
herself and Kirkby, although in point of fact it
was not yet in existence! Just by closing her eyes
she could see herself in it again; could feel, as
she had felt in the night, her pleasure in her
environment. It was a small house, of course,
with no more than four rooms in it, at the most,
but it was a smallness which made for comfort
and not constriction. She had felt so happy in
it, so snug, that she laughed contentedly at the
very remembrance. It was a queer thing, when
you came to think of it, and rather uncanny,
that you could feel at home in a house which
hadn't even been built!

There were more than four rooms in the cottage in which she had lived so long, but she had
always felt pressed in upon by it, and as if she
could hardly breathe. It was a good place, of
course, and a big one, as cottages went,—almost
too big, indeed, when it came to single-handed
work. But she had never yet felt at home in it,
or known the intimate joy of the home-lover and
the home-maker. She had done her duty by it,
that was all. She had lived and worked in it
merely as a caretaker might have lived and
worked, and, on the few occasions when she had

gone away from it, she had felt as if it had ceased
to exist. . . .

There was only one thing which had troubled
her in the dream, and she had not said anything
to Kirkby about it. Indeed, she had almost forgotten it when she awoke, safe in her hopes as
she was, as if ringed by shields; but now it set
her mind wondering and her brow wrinkling. . . .
She had been troubled and puzzled because of
the questions which They had asked her.

Maggie, for instance, had wanted to know all
about the people at home,—who lived in this
place and that, and a lot of other things which
she had been put to it to answer.

'Who's got Beck Edge, nowadays, Mother,
and Field Howe? Beck Edge belonged to the
father, didn't it, and t'other to the son? I remember hearing they wanted to change about,
but I don't know if they ever did.'

Her mother, however, had been quite unable
to clear up the mystery,—if mystery there was,
—about Beck Edge and Field Howe. She had
never been interested in the matter, and she
cared nothing about it now. But Maggie was so
interested that she couldn't stop talking about
it. Her colour rose and her eyes shone. Digging
up vague details from a quite improbable past,
she proceeded to shape them into an unreliable
present. You might almost have thought that
she had a personal bias in the affair; whereas the
truth was that she had never been nearer either
of the houses than a crow's flight on a fine day.

Luke's questions had been chiefly about the
staff,—who was working for his father, these
days, and what had happened to the rest. 'I

always thought Nicholson wouldn't last so long,'
he had said. 'He was a bad egg,—sure! Tommy
Rigg'll be getting an old man now, and likely
past his work. What? D'you mean to say he's
been gone five year back and more? Gosh!
How time does scoot!'

He had said another thing after that which
had annoyed her sorely in the dream, and which
even in remembrance made her fume a little.

'Len Machell's still hanging on, isn't he?' he
had asked. 'Father thought a lot of Len. I never
let on to you about it, Mother, but he once
applied to me for a job. When we were on our
feet, it was, and he knew we'd something to
offer; but of course I told him that I shouldn't
think of sniping him like that from the old dad.'

She had been pretty short with him, she remembered now,—had implied, whilst busy com-
menting upon Machell's 'cheek,' that there had
been 'cheek' on Luke's part, as well. He had
only laughed in his cheerful way, and the dream
had melted and changed, but the flame of her
indignation was still at work within her. She
had not known that she could care so much
about a thing like that, or that she could resent
so bitterly a slight on Kirkby. And not only
Kirkby himself, but Kirkby's job, which she had
always imagined that she despised and hated!
. . . She was surprised by her own attitude, and
lay for some time brooding over it. It was only
with difficulty that she reminded herself that it
was 'only a dream,' and that in all probability
Machell had never applied at all.

Joe's questions had been much the same as
Luke's, with now and then a family resemblance

to some of Maggie's. He, too, had wanted to know about the staff, and who was now at the Home Farm. But he had also wanted information about some of his old-time sweethearts, and that with his wife sitting by and not looking over-suited!

'Where's Bessie Dale, these days, Mother, and Carrie Sharpe? Married long since, both of them, I'll be bound,—nay, don't tell me you've never heard! Carrie was a school-teacher, you'll think on, and Bessie in Morton's office. There was Dolly Dale, as well, but, of course, *she* married Len Machell. . . .' It was queer how the Machells kept coming into the dream!

She had done her best to suppress Joe, both because of his wife's crab-apple look, and because of the hot little ache at the heart which mothers feel at the mention of girls who have wanted their sons. But he had refused to be silenced, at first, and had gone on chattering about Dolly. 'Dolly was the best of the bunch,' he had said, laughing, 'and more than a bit fond of yours truly. Len would never have got her, I know that, if I'd stopped at home instead of hitting the trail!'

But They had got tired at last of asking her about England,—even Joe, who saw it sunned by the bright smiles of his lost lasses. They had understood that she did not want to talk about it, and had stopped teasing her, realising also that she had very little to tell them. But it had been impossible to explain that it had ceased to be real to her as soon as she had left it,—that she had clean forgotten such things as that Machell had married Dolly!

It was Ellen, amazingly, who had been the worst of all, because it was Ellen who had asked about the house and gardens. This was the more surprising because she had been the one child who had seemed to share her mother's dislike of them. Many a pleasant chat they had had together, abusing the dull, shut-in place, and feeling greatly enlivened. And now it was Ellen who was bringing it back to mind, tying her down to it again when at last she was safely shot of it!

'Have you got that extra window put in, Mother, you were always so keen on? Does the kitchen fire still smoke in a west wind? Privet hedge'll have grown to a grand size, nowadays, I expect? Does the dad still grow "Creeping Jenny" over the front door?'

She had tried hard to find answers for Ellen, sitting on a stool at her knee, and fondly fingering her skirt. There had been a distant look in her eyes as she put her questions, as if her mind had jumped to her mother's side of the ocean, as her mother's had jumped to hers. Mattie had felt it a trifle disloyal of Ellen to have gone away, so to speak, the moment she arrived. It was almost as if they had been nearer together when those heaving miles of Atlantic had lain between them. . . .

But those were the only shadows which had blurred the exquisiteness of the dream, and the effect of them, after all, had been to make it even more real. For, as she had to admit, those were the very questions that They *would* ask, Over There, until their excitement over their parents' arrival had sobered down a little. Later on, too, they would ask, at intervals, again, for even in the busiest lives there are hours when, the body quiet, the mind insists upon travelling. But she would not mind it so much, then. . . . It was only Ellen who had given her something of a shock,— whose questions, now that she came to think of them, did not seem quite real.

The rest of the experience, however, had been pure joy, so full of laughter and sweet looks and tender touches that it seemed as if the sensation of them must last for ever. There were the grandchildren, too,—but she must give an hour or two, later, to thinking about them. They were too many, and too dear, to be hurried over when she ought to be getting up and seeing to Kirkby's breakfast.

But the biggest thing in the dream had been the feeling of escape,—together with that exhilarating sense of space after which she had always hankered, without rhyme or reason. Other places, no doubt, could have given her that same sense, but it was Canada that had captured her imagination. Canada as a whole seemed to have got into the dream, with its strong air, its mountains and lakes, and its long stretches of land reaching to the great line of its horizon. She thought of prairies and woods, and great rivers, and ice-bound harbours. She saw the glint of gold, and dog-sledges racing over frozen country. She saw the soft colours of ripened orchards, and a fresh wind running for miles over the stooping heads of wheat. . . . All that she had heard and read about the Dominion seemed to have merged into one single setting for that keen adventure of her spirit.

It had all been wonderful beyond imagining, joyful beyond ecstasy; perfect,—no, not quite perfect. There had been just one thing lacking, —one person who had not been present. Kirkby was not in the dream. . . .

II

SHE was still wondering why Kirkby was not
in the dream when she had got herself out of
bed and was beginning to dress quickly, although
not so quickly as she was in the habit of dressing,
for her limbs felt heavy, this morning, as if her
body also had travelled in the night. Her mind,
too, was still inclined to wander, so that at intervals she found herself losing touch with what she
was doing. In the very act of fastening button or
tape, sewn on with that rapid efficiency which
was her distinguishing characteristic, she would
pause to answer some question put by a voice
which could not be less than three thousand
miles away.

She felt disconcerted by the fact that Kirkby
had apparently had neither lot nor part in last
night's expedition. She was also rather glad,
with a queer, jealous gladness which she did
not understand, and which made her slightly
ashamed. But his absence not only detracted
from the reality of the dream; it rather frightened
her. The superstition always dormant at the
back of the country mind rose up to persuade her
that Kirkby would never live to cross the ocean
with her.

But the shadow soon passed, as the other
shadows had passed, and the rush of excitement
returned more headily than ever. She even sang
as she dressed, and then stopped with a laugh,
feeling that even the walls of the house must
come alive to hear her. She was the type of
woman who sings naturally as she moves about,

but the number of times she had sung in that house she could count on her ten fingers. . . . Not only had she not had the heart to sing in a place so hostile to her, but it would have seemed to her rather false, implying to all who might hear it that she was beginning to 'settle down.'

She had not known that she was going to dislike the place when she first came to it; indeed, she had never even thought about it. She had taken it for granted that she would 'settle,' as everybody else, apparently, settled. She had been too young, at that time, to know much about wives who wanted to 'move on,' although she had come across more than one (and thought nothing of them) in later life. And she had certainly not known that the place you lived in could be either your enemy or your friend.

Yet she might have guessed that it would not do for her to be dumped down just anywhere; that, like so many of Kirkby's precious plants, she needed a special soil on which to thrive. And at least she might have guessed that she needed room. . . . Quite early on, her mother had noticed the fact, and commented upon it.

'Look at her now,' Mattie could vaguely recall her saying, pointing her out to some on-looker as she sat at table, 'pushing and shoving at t' pots till she's got 'em away from her! She did the same as a babby, and a sight o' mugs she broke an' all! She can't abide to be cluttered up, or to have folks pressing on her, can't our Mattie.'

She had said the same to the school-teacher, when, calling indignantly to demand the meaning of some trifling punishment, she was told that

Mattie had insisted upon annexing more of the school-bench than she was entitled to.

'She'll never do as she's meant if you don't allow for it,' was her parting advice. 'Best give her two folks' room, and then you'll have done with it. She's a big child, to begin with,—as fine a one as you'll see anywhere, though I says it as shouldn't,—but it isn't only that. It's just she can't do with feeling she hasn't room to breathe and spread about in.'

Later on, of course, she had learned to adapt herself better to the conditions in which she lived, so that pots were no longer broken, or schoolfellows thrust aside. But her love of space continued to grow with her, although more or less unconsciously, showing itself mainly in a liking for long walks, and for open windows and doors. It was during a dispute with her mother over the latter that for once she had caught a faint glimpse of the life for which she was really intended. An aunt of hers had been staying with them, who knew a little of the world, and she had taken a hand in the family quarrel.

'Folks can't all think the same,' she had said, in reply to the mother's statement that 'if our Mattie had her way, roof would be off afore you could say Jack Robinson!' 'They're different, all the world over. Your Mattie 'd likely do rarely in one o' them new countries they're talking of opening up.'

Mattie's mother had been altogether vague upon the subject of 'new countries,' having, indeed, sufficient difficulty, as it was, in realising that there was more of England beyond the one little spot in which she lived and moved and had her being. . . . 'Eh, now! What countries?' she had enquired incredulously, rather as if she suspected the visitor of inventing them on the spur of the moment.

'Colonies, they call 'em,' the other had said firmly, although almost equally vaguely, and speaking the word as people spoke it in those days, before such names as Canada and New Zealand had become living realities to the public mind. 'Fine big spots wanting big strong folk as like fresh air and a bit o' work. Your Mattie 'd do grand for Colonies, from what they tell me.'

'They're big, d'you say?' Mattie herself had asked, fixing upon the one point which had intrigued her imagination, and, in that one word, had she but known it, assessing the whole of her life's trouble.

The visitor nodded.

'Big, every way, so I understand. Mountains and rivers, and great pieces as they call—nay, I can't think on, except that I know it made me think o' church. Trouble is, though, they're such a sight of a long way off,—t'other side of the ocean, though I'm sure I can't say which.'

Mattie's mother had laughed when the ocean was mentioned, as though the very sound of that awe-inspiring word had put a full stop to the conversation.

'Nay, now, it's no use your talking Colonies to the lass, if there's oceans and such-like mixed up in it! She can't abide the sea, can't our Mattie, and never could. I don't know where she gets it from, I'm sure, unless it's my mother, as was once right near drowned, falling off a pier at Morecambe. She had a terble down on the sea, after that, and I reckon our Mattie's the same. What, she can't even abide a picture of it in the room,—says it puts her off her meat! Nay, if Colonies means crossing the ocean and such-like, I reckon they'll have to do without our Mattie.'

Remembering this speech of her mother, ominously clear as speeches seem which have been long forgotten and then are suddenly recalled, she felt disconcerted for the second time, that morning. It was true, of course, that she had always dreaded the sea. Every kind of evil of which it was capable had seemed at one time or another to fasten upon her imagination. Accounts of shipwrecks held her as no other literature had power to hold her,—tidal waves, broken embankments, water-spouts moving like monstrous spectres. . . . The sea was the only thing in life which had so far been able to intimidate her, and she had not yet mastered her fear of it. Not easily would she forget those bad days after her children had sailed, or the unbelievable relief with which she had heard that the ground was firm again under their feet.

And now she was definitely committed to cross that very ocean which had driven the Colonies out of a cottage talk all those years ago! Even in the midst of her luminous satisfaction she shivered as she remembered it. The sea frightened you, made you sick, heaved you about, and then finally drowned you. . . . Not, of course, that she anticipated being drowned,—the dream alone seemed surety enough for that—but she knew that she would suffer it a hundred times in her mind before she was safely landed.

Yet it had to be faced if ever she was to know
the happiness that was waiting for her, Over
There. . . . She felt a pang of impatience because
she could not make the journey as she had just
made it in the night,—as she had made it many
and many a time over her cooking or her needle.
Yet, what were a few days of misery, after all,
compared with the long heart-breaking years
through which she had struggled already?

The picture called up by her aunt had faded
as soon as it was painted, not only blotted out
by the terrors of the sea, but dwindling from
sheer vagueness. She had had that one hint of
a door wider than any of those which she opened
daily, and then it was closed again before she
could see beyond it. One glimpse, followed by
a single pang of recognition and disappointment
. . . and presently she had forgotten it. In any
case, she would have had little use for the
Colonies, just then, for already she was aware
that she meant to marry Kirkby.

Looking back, she could see him coming into
her life as softly as the river mists which lay so
often upon the gardens, and which she so much
dreaded and hated. She could not remember
either the day she had first met him, or the still
more important day when he had asked her to
marry him. All that she knew was that he had
not been in her life, and then suddenly he was
all of it. She could no more trace the moment
when that had happened than she had ever been
able to catch a tulip closing for the night.

She had neither hated nor dreaded Kirkby,
in spite of his home mists, and even now the
memory of their courtship had the power to

thrill her with its sweetness. But he had been the wrong mate for her, nevertheless. He and all that he represented had muffled her spirit as the mists had muffled her body. The bold driving-force that was in her had been irritated by his reserved and delicate ways. It was amazing that they had pulled together as well as they had,— she always reaching outward, and he always holding back. Many a couple as badly suited would have parted company before now.

She winced a little in her new happiness, remembering how often she had felt bitterly towards him. She was ashamed, now, of their many quarrels. . . . In the great peace that had come to her it seemed impossible that there could ever have been anything but peace. Even when they were not disputing, she had raged against him in her heart. She flushed as she recalled that she had actually sunk so low as to try to set the children against him. . . .

She flushed and she was ashamed, but these troubles out of the past had already vanished so far that they could not really hurt the present. Already they were gone as the wrinkles in a cloth were gone as soon as a hot iron was passed upon them. With the new peace had come to her also a new vision. She had not meant to hurt Kirkby any more than he had meant to hurt her. She would do her best to make up to him for it in the little time that was left to them Over There.

It seemed strange to her now that her mother, who had read her so plainly when she was small, had yet not seen fit to warn her when she most required it. Perhaps she was one of those people who could see things clearly in a child, but never thought about them again directly they grew up. Even if she had thought, she would only have said that a good husband like Kirkby was not to be sneezed at. Mattie herself would have said it, if a child of her own had asked her. He was a decent, steady young man in a job to which she was accustomed. You did not sneeze at a man like that if you had any sense of values.

She had not sneezed at him, and she was not sneezing now, though she had sneezed often enough at what he had had to offer. It was a better position, of course, than might well have fallen to her lot; a better one, for instance, than had fallen to her sisters. It was not Kirkby's fault that the longing with which she had been born had finally got on her mind; and it was certainly her fault, if it was anybody's, that the children had been born with it, too!

She opened the window before going downstairs, her glance falling, as she did so, on the privet hedge, and she was amazed by the sudden rush of affection which took her as she looked at it. The shadows were still on the little lawn which it sheltered, giving it that air of seclusion for which it had been planned. A flower-bed ran all round the lawn under the hedge, and in the middle of the grass was another bed with a standard rose. At one end of the little plot was a rustic seat, set with its back to the rest of the gardens and its face towards the west.

The Mattie looking out of the window saw many Matties walking in that little plot, and making it, by dint of years of dreaming, into an orchard of escape. She saw a young Mattie, first of all, and a little hedge, too thin and too small to fend off the curious glances of the men working close at hand. But the years fled before her mind little faster than they had fled in actual truth. Almost before you could turn round there was an older Mattie and an older hedge, with flowers in the trim border and a green closeness about the lawn. And presently both Mattie and the hedge were growing old and stout, and the turf had grown thick and soft, and there was a snug richness about the soil. . . .

The little place, where, as she had told Kirkby, she was able to 'get away,' had very soon become the real centre of her married life. To it she had taken both her early discontent and her later bitterness of frustration. Many a hard speech, which otherwise might have been Kirkby's portion, had been tossed off at the privet hedge; many a salt tear had been wept into that lawn! Sitting and sewing in it, she had been a girl again, in her home towards the west. Walking in it, with her Canadian letters in her hand, the tiny spot had resolved itself into that broad country where her soul went free.

Going to Canada would, of course, mean leaving that little home of memories behind her. Somebody else would have the right to walk in it, to sit and sew and dream. . . . She felt a jealousy that was almost fierce as she thought of that somebody, and her throat contracted a little. If it had been possible, she would have gathered up the lawn and the privet hedge, and taken them away with her.

She continued to feel amazed by her sudden feeling for the place; or, rather, by the sudden revelation that it meant so much to her. She had thought of it only as a refuge, a makeshift for want of anything better, and now it had become something that actually belonged to her. She tested herself, looking away from it and then back to it again, and felt always the same rush of affection and the same jealous ache. She had always thought that she hated every inch of the ground on which her married life had been spent; but in spite of herself these few square yards of it had stolen into her heart.

Perhaps it was only, she thought, that the place looked different because she was leaving it. It was a well-known fact that people often regretted even the worst of things when the time came for them to part with them. (Why, she had had a cousin of her own with a broken leg, who had cried when her crutches had been taken away from her!) Or else it was just because she had not been free that she had not been able to see things properly. It was her mind, even more than her body, that had been in chains, and now she had shaken the chains from her. Perhaps she was seeing things now as she would see them in Canada, when at last she had got away from them. . . .

She went downstairs, still thinking about the privet hedge, and feeling her first ecstasy a little tarnished. She knew now, what she had not realised before, that, in spite of the joy that was coming, there were things that would make her suffer. She had fondly imagined that she had paid for the joy long since, but apparently she had been wrong. Life was piling its debts against you all the time. . . . Already there had been the questions and the thought of the sea; and now had come the shock of the privet hedge. They would plant another hedge for her, if she wanted it, Over There, but they could not ensure her another forty years in which to watch it growing. They could not make each leaf and twig speak to the memories of a whole life. They could not give her back the English soil which she had salted and watered with her tears.

III

Bᴜᴛ even before she set foot in the kitchen her mind had recovered its tone. The mere fact of rapid movement, of swift passage from one room to another, had, as always, the power to cheer her. As for the letter, the presence of which had so intimidated Kirkby that it had taken him at least half an hour to look at it, she found it little less than a magic spell. To see it lying there on the table was almost to hear her children's voices bidding her good morning, to meet their faces turned towards her as she entered, and to feel the warm reality of their hands.

So far, at least, Kirkby had not repented of his decision, she thought, relieved, finding a fresh resting-place for the precious object. He had let the letter lie. . . . It was true, of course, that he had seemed to have no regrets when he came to her upstairs, but you could not always tell. There was time, as she had just proved, for a whole change of heart between the first stair and the last. And he had never really wanted to go, in spite of his hankering after that distant garden and a fresh sight of his lads.

He had never yet broken a promise to her that she could remember; yet she knew that she would feel a good deal happier when the letter had really gone. For a moment she thought of stamping it and giving it to the postman, if he should happen to call, but abandoned the idea instantly. Kirkby, as she knew, would prefer to give it in by hand. In these out-of-the-way places it was still considered insulting to persons of high degree to send them a letter of that sort through the post.

There would be other letters for the post, anyhow, she thought gleefully, as she prepared breakfast. Letters to her sisters, telling them that she was leaving England . . . to one or two old friends still surviving in the neighbourhood of her home. Letters about passages and passports . . . about her single tiny investment. . . . Above all, the great letter to Them, Over There, announcing their speedy coming.

She would write to Luke, she supposed, he being not only the eldest of the family, but the head of the firm. It was to his house that they would probably go, until their own could be got ready for them. But she had it at the back of her mind that she would write to Ellen, as well. Ellen was the one who would be the most pleased about it, she thought fondly, if it was fair to say that any one of them would be more pleased than the others.

The phrasing of the letter, some of it new, but most of it so old as to have become almost mechanical, raced and hammered through her brain to a triumphant close, only to begin again the moment it was finished. Always she saw it written, not in ink, but in scrolled and burnished gold; with certain extracts, such as 'see you again,' 'really coming,' and 'hoping to find you as this leaves me,' rising above the rest like rocks in a golden sea.

She had had moments when she had thought that a quieter method would be more appropriate to the occasion,—a few, quiet, colourless sentences, easily filled in by those to whom they were sent. She had waited so long and so bitterly that it seemed almost indecent to make a song about it. . . . But now that the time had actually arrived she was too happy to be restrained and tasteful. The only letter that would satisfy her would be vivid and underlined, with exclamation-marks scattered here and there like little shouts of joy.

The quieter method, however, would do excellently for her sisters and the few old friends. Too great a show of excitement would seem out of place to them. They would sympathise, of course, with her desire to see her children, but otherwise they would be sure to think that she was making a mistake. Folks who never moved more than a yard from their own spots all their lives always did think that others who moved a yard or two farther were making a mistake.

In any case, they had always been inclined to think her 'a bit wild,' although why it should be considered 'wild' to want to live in one country rather than another it was difficult to see. Anyhow, it was lucky for the Empire that somebody had been wild enough to do it sometimes! Occasionally she had tried to point this out both to the sisters and the friends, but she had never convinced them that it applied to her personally. Perhaps the folks among whom you were brought up never did understand that things might apply to you just as much as to the people outside.

No doubt the neighbours here had thought her 'a bit wild,' too, and discussed her disapprovingly over their tea-cups. The village was a small one, little more than a hamlet set on the edge of the park, and no member of the limited community would be likely to escape its gossip. The thought of their shaken heads did not distress her, however, for she had found them a kindly enough lot, on the whole. More than one of them would have a good word for her, she knew, when the message got round to them that she was leaving them for ever.

She had known some of them now for nearly forty years, and yet there was not one among them she could really call a friend. They were on good enough terms, of course,—such terms as other people would undoubtedly call friendship; but in this, as in other things, she had asked more of life than it had so far seen fit to give her. A friend was a person you settled down with, side by side, and whose life dovetailed into yours as board dovetailed into board. She had never been able to have a friend like that because she had never been able to settle down. Always she had lived like someone starting on a journey, for whom at any moment the signal may be dropped.

It was not only that, in her first years of homesickness and revolt, she had not cared to know the people in the place; or that, having come from a village which was the hereditary enemy of this, she was naturally disposed to dislike its inhabitants. There was jealousy between villages as bitter and lasting as there ever was between individuals. Nobody knew what started it, as a rule, or why it persisted from generation to generation. But, the moment the people from these two places happened to get together, there was bound to be trouble. Before you could turn

round, they were at work belauding themselves
and belittling each other, whether it was about
football or the quality of the land or the amount
of money in the Sunday collection-bag.

Kirkby had been not only too gentle but too
much in love to make trouble of that kind,
although she herself had made it unashamedly
in their quarrels. But that particular feeling of
animosity had died in her to some extent as time
went on. The real bar to friendship had been the
fear of being tied down,—the necessity for keeping
herself free against the hour when she should go.

Well, she had not tied herself down, and for all
those years of keeping herself aloof from people
she would find herself repaid. There would be
no tears on either side when the time came to
say good-bye. She would be able to slip away
without bitterness or regret, without a single pull
at her heart, or a hand snatching at her own.

She would be sorry to part with some of them,
all the same, even though there would be no
sharpness about the sorrow. Things came back
to her now which had long since dropped away,
but which had touched her nearly, at the time.
Kindnesses, which, for the time being, at least,
had seemed to make life brighter. . . . Gifts, with
the kind of thought behind them that was better
than any gift. . . . Jokes, which had stayed persistently in her mind, and made a sort of laughter
here, even if it could not reach her lips.

And other things, infinitely more poignant,
which, impossible as it seemed, she was beginning to forget. . . . That year when Ellen had
nearly died, and Mrs. Grisedale had come un-
asked to help her with the nursing. . . . She could

still see her face as she bent over the sick child, could hear the note in her voice to which, as to an actual arm, both she and Ellen had clung. She had done her best to repay the kindness, although she had not maintained the intimacy, and she had thought the matter cleared. But she knew now that, when the time came for saying good-bye to Mrs. Grisedale, she would also have to say good-bye to the bitter-sweet memory of which she was a part.

The things which you did for others were even worse in rising up against you at farewell moments. . . . It was she herself to whom Mrs. Ellwood had clung, during those first bad weeks after the poor thing had lost her husband. Ignoring her own people, she had asked firmly for Mattie, and Mattie had gone to her, as one always did go, in these cases. They had drifted apart long since, but they would remember when she said good-bye. . . . She felt absurdly that she was in some way forsaking Mrs. Ellwood, even though for twenty years at least they had been nothing more to each other than just ordinary good neighbours.

No doubt she would have other if lesser pangs to bear before she was finished with her acquaintance. Of course, it was open to her to go without saying good-bye at all, but she was not willing to slink off as if ashamed of what she was doing. The pangs would be lost soon enough in the happiness ahead of her. But she saw once again that, no matter what you paid, there was always something to pay. No matter how you kept yourself free of life, life would never leave you free. . . .

IV

SHE passed with a sigh of relief to the thought
of all that would have to be done before she
could get away. Her heart rose to the task as she
remembered it. Work,—and especially organis-
ing work,—had always been a pleasure to her,
and this would mean more than pleasure. In
the rush of planning and packing, of solving the
many problems which would undoubtedly arise,
she would easily lose sight of the few burdens
that were weighing on her spirit.

At the moment, however, she had no intention of beginning to pull the house to pieces, or
even of starting upon such minor operations as
going through drawers and cupboards. There
would be no sense in making the place uncomfortable before she was obliged. The day would
be full enough, as it was, what with the ordinary
routine and the letters which had to be written;
not to speak of the long hours of dreaming
and gloating to which she would certainly fall
captive.

There would be plenty to do, of course, when
the moment arrived, but it would be done all
right, and done like so much clockwork. In any
case, her house, always in order and always
clean, was not the sort that had almost to be
built over again before it was fit to leave. It was
not overcrowded, either, with those things which
accumulate as the years go on; so unconsciously,
sometimes, that they seem to have grown out of
the very stuff of life itself. Broadly speaking, she
was almost as free of unnecessary belongings

as a seabird poised for flight on the edge of a naked cliff.

Yet, almost without knowing what she was doing, she was setting her hand to the lever which Fate had so tardily thrust into it. Even while she was making the breakfast she was moving a few things here and there, rejecting this and accepting that, and hunting for paper and string with which to pack them. It was more than likely that they would have to be unpacked again, later on; even if, in a future scheme of things, they were not left behind altogether. But the excitement of putting the work in train was impossible to resist. With each parcel she packed, her heart rose a little higher. Every change in the standing order of things was an added assurance that that order was at an end.

The desire to alter it even further grew upon her when breakfast was over and Kirkby had returned to his duties. A great restlessness possessed her. It was almost as if the long strain of waiting for what she wanted had sapped her power to believe in it when it came; as if she feared that, unless she instantly took advantage of it, it might still manage to evade her. . . .

It was this fear that drove her to shifting the furniture, to dragging out hidden treasures, and reducing the house generally to a chaotic state worse even than in the yearly whirlpool of spring-cleaning. Pushing and tugging, she performed feats of strength which she had thought beyond her, even in youth, and which sent her gasping to a chair for a few moments' relaxation. She raced up and down stairs fetching and carrying, and then did not know what to do with things, and had to take them back again. The tide of life within her rose to its fullest height in the necessity for proving to herself that at last the longed-for miracle had been accomplished.

She was standing on a chair by the dresser, measuring the pot-rail with a tape, and in constant danger of losing her balance in her efforts, when the postman's whistle came shrilling up to her as he climbed towards the gardens. In the sudden start that it gave her she lost count of what she was doing, and, getting down rather stiffly, she went to the door to wait for him.

For how many years now, she said to herself, still flushed and panting, had she listened, morning by morning, for Dick Nelson's whistle! For how many years now had it had power to thrill her, carrying with it, as it so often did, the possibility of a Canadian letter! Even when there was no chance of such a thing it could set her heart leaping and her eyes shining. The single, climbing note of it had always been for her a call straight from the Great Beyond.

So many mornings she had longed and listened, and now she could almost count on her fingers the mornings that were left! She wondered whether she would still find herself listening when she was over the water,—going to the door, perhaps, to stand waiting and watching. It would be some time, no doubt, before she would get used to doing without those constant letters. She had lived for them so long that the loss of them at first would be almost like the loss of meat and drink.

She would not need them, of course, when she

had the children,—so much nearer and dearer than any letter could make them!—but she would miss them, all the same. There were things people told you in letters which they never told in the flesh; things they felt for you when they wrote which they did not think of when you were by. And, once written, you had them to turn to, even if they never said them again. The very handwriting of those who loved you was in itself a loving speech. . . .

The postman was getting nearer now, she could tell, and he had not whistled again. He had known for many a year now that he did not need to whistle more than once when it came to Mrs. Kirkby! . . . Like a wise man, he was saving his breath for the last steep little pull that led to the gardens. She could hear him wheezing and puffing, as it was, and the shuffle of his step which betrayed the slow lifting of his feet. Dick Nelson was getting old, she thought idly, and then remembered with a start that he was the same age as herself. She knew that was so because he had told her his age on his last birthday, and, looking at his wrinkles and his bowed back, she had been startled, even then. To-day, listening to his puffing and pausing as he climbed the garden path, she was more than startled. To-day, faced as she was with new conditions that would make such trial of her strength, Dick's loss of vigour seemed an actual menace.

She tried to console herself with the thought that age was purely a personal matter, and that people did not necessarily grow old at the same rate because they were born on the same day. Dick, as she knew, had been a weakling in his

youth, whereas she had never known ache or
pain. A walking-post's job was a trying one, too,
especially in this northern climate. . . . Nevertheless, she found it an effort to look at him as
he came in at the little gate.

He was still wheezing as he stopped in front
of her, and, diving into his bag, produced a flat
packet, which she saw to be addressed to her
in Ellen's writing. He fumbled a little with it
before he handed it over, and, for the moment,
curiously enough, she felt no impulse to take it
from him.

'Another letter from your folks, Missis,' Dick
said, with the familiarity of the old country postman, which pays for itself by a genuine sympathy
in either joy or sorrow. 'It should ha' been here
yesterday, but I took it to Mrs. Crosby's, by
mistake.'

Mattie looked rather vexed at that, both because she did not like Mrs. Crosby, and because
she was unaccountably troubled by the sudden
appearance of the packet.

'I should think it *was* a mistake!' she answered
him rather sharply, though at the same time
trying to tone down her reproof for the sake of
old acquaintance. 'There's not much likeness
between Kirkby and Crosby that I can see!'

'Nay, nor between the folks, neither!' Dick
chuckled, setting her flushing again, though now
it was from flattered vanity instead of anger.
Mrs. Crosby was a thin little rat of a woman,
with a red head and a blue nose,—about as different a person from Mattie as you could find in
a day's march. . . . Dick might be stupid and
short of breath, she reflected, softening, but he

still knew a fine woman when he came across one.

'It's my eyes, d'ye see?' he was saying, when she attended to him again, and emphasising his remarks with sharp flaps of the Canadian packet. 'I'll have to be seeing about getting glasses. Anyhow, the letter's here all right, and none the worse for a bit of extra travelling. . . . It'll be a likeness, I reckon, from the look of it,' he finished, handing it to her at last with an air of making a concession.

It probably *was* a likeness, Mattie told him, holding it in her hands with the same curious sense of reluctance in her fingers. She might have told him more but for that remark of his about his eyes, reminding her as it did of the increasing disadvantages of age. Dick had seen many a snapshot of her family in his time, and had not thought twice about giving his own opinion of them, either. . . . 'My folks Over There are always sending me something to look at.'

'They'll not be sending much longer, if all tales is true!' Dick's eyes seemed keen enough now, as they lifted themselves, twinkling. 'There's barely a house I call at but somebody asks me when Mrs. Kirkby's off to Canada!'

Mattie laughed in return, but with a slight nervousness that surprised her. She had only to mention the 'notice,' and the whole place would be agog; making it, with every reference to the subject, more certain and more 'real.' But something, which she took to be loyalty to Kirkby, held her back from speaking. 'Ay, well, and what d'you say to that?' she compromised, by way of answer.

Dick shifted his bag and shuffled his feet, finally clearing his throat like one preparing for an oration.

'Well, if you want to know, ten year ago I said you'd be off as sharp as a dog to its kennel. Five year ago, I said—"Ay, well, less likely things has happened." But, to-day, when they ax me, I say I wouldn't believe it even if I was to see it.'

The colour rose higher yet in Mattie's face, but the thing that lay close in her heart was too warm for a show of temper.

'Whatever makes you say that?' she queried innocently.

For the first time Dick showed signs of discomfort, turning about a little, and looking away from her. 'Nay, it's just that you're not so young, these days,' he returned at last, bravely. 'Same age as myself, I've heard my old mother say, and you'd not catch *me* crossing t' ocean if you give me Canada!'

'Folks are as young as they feel,' Mattie said, trying to repress the pang which had seized her when he mentioned the ocean. 'The sea's nothing to me! As for age and such-like, there's folks go abroad when they're a deal older than us. What, I remember Mrs. Dugdale going off to New Zealand when she was nigh on ninety!'

'Ay, but they go sudden-like,' Dick said, wrinkling his brow as if to help the working of his brain. 'They don't sit planning a sight o' years. Things is sudden-like when they're meant.'

'Things always seem sudden when they come,' Mattie retorted briskly. 'Planning makes no difference. Look how folks know they're going to die from the very minute they're born, and yet they're mighty surprised about it when it happens!'

'Folks don't plan to die. . . . Leastways, them as does seldom brings it off. And that brings me back like to what I was trying to say. If you stop over long on the edge of a jump you take root afore you think.'

'I shan't have much root to bother about if I go to Canada!' Mattie laughed. 'Saving your presence, Mr. Nelson, there's precious little I'd mind leaving behind.'

The old postman shook his head.

'You strike roots afore you know. Everything as you do each day is a root o' some sort. Even folks as has been in prison knows what it is to strike roots.'

The privet hedge came into Mattie's mind, together with that past look on Mrs. Grisedale's face, and the clinging touch of Mrs. Ellwood's hand. . . . But she laughed again.

'They're roots as is easy pulled up, I should say!' she said cheerfully. 'Folks in prison, I mean. . . . As for me, I've always been on the go, so to speak. I've never settled down.'

'You can't *not* settle!' Dick said suddenly, in a loud voice that was almost threatening. 'Don't you make any mistake, Mrs. Kirkby. Life settles you. Time settles you. You can't *not* settle!'

The annoyance she had been keeping in check rose at that to a strong head, but it was succeeded almost at once by a feeling of pity. Dick looked so old, standing there, weighed down by his heavy bag, and with the fine spring sunlight showing up his wrinkles. He was jealous, she said to herself, because he felt old, and because, perhaps, he, too, had wanted to go to Canada. She could have laughed now at the thought that they were the same age. In the pride of her new joy she felt like a girl beside him,—a girl with her strength to draw at, and the whole wide world before her.

'Ay, well, I don't see as we need quarrel about it,' she said amiably. 'Likely what you say's right most of the time, if it isn't always. Anyway, Canada or no Canada, it's a bonny morning!'

But Dick was already shambling away towards the office, wheezing as he went, and grumbling to himself as an old dog grumbles when he meets a young one. She smiled as she saw him stumble over a stone, and stop in a rage to kick it from him. Thrusting the letters in at the office with a shaky hand, he swung about crossly and disappeared round a corner of the building.

V

WITH the smile still on her lips, Mattie turned herself round and went back into the kitchen. Dick was a grumpy old thing, she thought cheerfully, and, like many other old people, firmly convinced that his dismal view of life was the only possible one. But she could not help feeling sorry that he had gone away in a rage. On a day that should have been joy from dawn to set, she did not like to think that she had had even the shadow of a dispute with such an old acquaintance.

She would miss Dick's constant visits when she had got to the other side, his grumpiness and his whistle, and his rough, outspoken comments. It would be a bit of a nuisance, too, to have to get used to dealing with new tradespeople. Shopfolk took a lot of getting to know, wherever you happened to be, but she had long since got the better of hers. The grocer would never dream, nowadays, of sending her any but the right bacon, the right sugar, the right tea. As for the butcher, he had long ago given up trying to palm off on her any piece of meat except the one that she happened to ask for. It was a triumph to have got as far as that with a butcher, as anybody could tell you, and one that could hardly be achieved twice within the limits of a lifetime. She had a distinct feeling of dismay when she thought of having to start again with a fresh butcher.

Ellen's packet was still in her hand, and she stood looking down at it without attempting to

open it. For the first time in her life she had
not been altogether pleased to see Ellen's handwriting, and she could not understand it. At
sight of it she had had a sensation of interference
affecting her almost to physical recoil. She had
been so near to her children during the night that
a message arriving so soon afterwards seemed
bound to break the spell. Nor was the position
bettered by the fact that the packet ought to have
reached her the day before. There was something casual yet calculated about its coming this
morning which seemed to jar the serene procession of ordained events. Ellen ought to have
known, she found herself saying senselessly, that
after last night there was no need to keep sending
packets any more.

It was a photograph that she held, she felt
sure of that, and one for which she had long been
waiting. Among the many snapshots arriving
year by year there had never been one of Ellen,
arm in arm with a husband, or half hidden behind a baby. She had never 'taken' well, even in
her youth, and, once over the water, had firmly
refused to be 'taken' at all. Always she had resisted her mother's demands in that light, laughing way of hers which seemed to bring her so
closely to you. No photograph, so Mattie had
often felt, could possibly seem more real than the
Ellen who came to you with her letters.

She had continued to ask for one, nevertheless,
and at long last had come the news that it would
shortly be forthcoming. Ellen had written an
amusing account of her visit to the photogra-
pher's and of her sufferings during the proceed-
ings. The result, however, it seemed, had been

an unexpected success, and should presently be forwarded to her mother. Mattie had watched for that precious packet as a hen waits and watches for a hatching chicken. She could not have been more thrilled, she sometimes thought, if it had been Ellen herself who was coming through the post!

That excitement had paled now beside the vividness of the dream, as well as the greater interest of the new position. She looked at the parcel with indifference, almost with dislike . . . certainly with impatience, as at a thing come at the wrong time. She would open it later on, she said to herself, as she laid it down, and returned with a lightened heart to her measuring of the dresser.

Passing from that to other even more entrancing speculations, she was soon wrapped again in the atmosphere which Dick and the packet between them had temporarily dispelled. She forgot them both as she toiled and planned, stopping every now and then to remember Kirkby's dinner. Strung up though she was, and therefore sensitive to the least touch of trouble, she was still too high on the wave of success to be disheartened for long together.

Even when she had begun her absurd game with the furniture, that childish but charming pretence in the midst of which Machell had come upon her, she had not remembered the photograph. Moving again in the dream, she was able to turn even blocks of wood into the dear ones who had peopled it, so that they could scarcely have been more real to her if they had been present in the flesh. The little stool in her arms had held the warmth of a living child; the grandfather's clock had been more surely Ellen than the packet she had put away.

The sight of Machell smiling in at the door had no power to disillusion her. Machell did not annoy her, as Dick had done, by over-cocksure assertions that it was now too late to change. On the contrary, he was full of encouragement and congratulation, and anxious to know her plans. You would almost have thought, she said to herself, chuckling, that he was as glad of the move to Canada as she was herself!

Her spirits mounted still further as the sun mounted, and the day grew in clarity and beauty. Like all country-bred folk, she was susceptible to the influence of the weather, even when she was not consciously aware of it. Even when she was most withdrawn in mind from the atmosphere around her, she was still swayed by its many changes. The coming-out of the sun was a trumpet-call to her vitality, even if the note that it sounded was one of clamorous rebellion. A grey day had the power to chill her passion almost to fainting, even if neither it nor any other-coloured day was able to slay it altogether.

In her state of heightened sensibility she could not have failed to notice the conditions about her, but there was a good deal more to it than that. The miraculous way in which the barriers between herself and the place seemed to have broken down continued to surprise her. Now, when she looked out, she had a distinct sensation of pleasure, as well as that warmth of recognition which comes from loved association. It seemed impossible to her now that she could ever have regarded her home with horror and dislike. The garden walls and the paths gave her a sense of satisfaction which seemed to have the satisfaction of many years behind it. The tree-tops against the sky produced a thrill of joy suggesting a long chain of similarly sweet moments.

It was the same with the house, which she had so long thought of as a prison, and which had suddenly become a place of pleasantness and peace. For the first time in forty years she realised it as peculiarly and joyfully her own. She felt an impulse to sing as she saw the sunlight lying across the kitchen floor. Up in her bed-room the flowered wallpaper was printed with memories, like a book.

She did not know whether to be glad or sorry about the change, but it continued to amaze her. She tested it, as she had tested her sudden view of the privet hedge, and found that it stood it, as the privet hedge had stood it. Room after room she found rich and filled with the actual makings of her life. Each time that she went to window or house-door, she saw the view before her shine and smile.

It was while she was standing at the door during one of these pauses for mingled puzzle and rest that she saw Mrs. Machell coming across the gardens. Mrs. Machell was a plump little woman, full of bustle and talk, but there was a lilt about her to-day which she had never hither-to noticed. Also she looked from side to side of her as she came as if the place interested her more than usual. The spring must have got into Mrs. Machell's blood, Mattie thought, adding the head-turning and the lilt to the rest of her new puzzle.

It was some time, however, before the visitor actually reached the house. Coming upon Len at work among the raspberry canes, she stopped to talk to him, and they stood laughing and chatting together for several minutes. Mattie frowned a little as she watched them, seeing the fine spring day going and Kirkby's best work-man idling. But she was still too happy to be annoyed by a thing which, after all, was hardly within her province, and she had nothing but smiles for Len's wife when she finally approached her.

'It was good of you to come,' she began blithely, as she led the way into the kitchen. 'I didn't look for you so soon. There's not that much doing, yet awhile, of course, but I'm fair aching for someone to talk to!'

Mrs. Machell laughed as she looked about her at the chaotic state of things which had so dis-gusted Kirkby. She was a fine, bright little thing, Mattie thought, and Joe might have done worse than marry her. Her cheeks were still fresh, and the gold of her hair shone as she took off her hat in a business-like manner. She was the same age as Joe, too, which meant a couple of years older than Ellen. . . . Mattie joined in the laugh with the heartiness of the excellent housewife, who, for once in a lifetime, is found wanting.

'Ay, it looks like it, I'm sure,' she agreed, in reply to Mrs. Machell's remark that at all events there seemed plenty to be going on with. 'I'll be right grateful if you'll help me to put things straight. Kirkby was that sick about 'em at dinner, it fair went to your heart to see him!

A man minds a house being pulled about a deal more than a woman.'

'They do that!' Dolly Machell nodded wisely. 'They make as much noise about it as a dog being skifted from its kennel. I daren't so much as move a chair in our spot but Len's as uneasy as an earthquake!'

Mattie felt a prick in her pride that an under-gardener should presume to indulge in the same idiosyncrasies as distinguished Kirkby, but she covered it hastily. 'Ay, well, men must be men,' she returned kindly, generously admitting Len into at least that one category.

'I'd a feeling I must be doing something right off,' she went on, conscious that the general upset needed some explanation. 'Of course, I know it's over early yet to be arranging about the sale, but it won't be trouble wasted. I know a deal better where I am than when I started in at things, this morning.'

Mrs. Machell stole a glance at her in the chair into which she had sunk after taking her visitor into the kitchen. Mattie was hardly conscious that she had sat down, or that she was beginning to feel the effects of the work and excitement of the morning. But, to Mrs. Machell, weariness was written plain in the lines of her flushed face and the droop of her broad shoulders. Loose strands of her hair were straying wildly across her forehead. Her hands, resting heavily in her lap, looked older than the rest of her.

'Then you're really thinking of leaving, Mrs. Kirkby?' Dolly asked, with a casualness assumed to hide an inward tremor. 'Len said it was as certain as rent-day, but I said I didn't believe it.'

There came over Mattie the same reluctance to commit herself to a definite statement as she had felt when Dick's hinting had put a similar question. Indeed, now that she came to think of it, she had not been definite even with Len. He had assumed certain things, that was all, and she had allowed him to assume them. It was only to herself and to Kirkby that she had so far put into straight words the great fact of their going.

'Well, it looks like it, I'll give you that!' she answered good-temperedly, though with a touch of discomfort. 'I'll admit it looks like it. . . . But I don't know that it does to go shouting things out over soon. There's some think you'll likely spoil your luck that way if you're not careful.'

Dolly looked a little disconcerted for a moment, and then laughed brightly.

'Ay, well, we'll pretend it's true, shall we?' she said cheerfully. 'Just make a game of it? *That* can't spoil your luck! We'll pretend you're off to Canada, though you're stopping on just as usual.'

'That's it!' Mattie said, in a tone of obvious relief. 'We'll just pretend. . . . Well, then, my lass, if you want to know, we're thinking of getting away by nigh on the first boat that can take us.'

'Eh, now, if that isn't news!' Dolly played up promptly, for all the world as if she had never heard a suggestion of such a thing until that moment. Her face glowed as she spoke, and a faint astonishment took Mattie, as it had taken her with Len, that anybody else should care so much about the project. . . .

'But you can't get away that soon, can you?'

the younger woman went on. 'There's your
notice to give in, and folks to tell on the other
side. You'll be having a sale, you said; there'll
be that to settle. And likely there'll be a thing
or two you'll be wanting for the journey.'

Mattie felt a fresh twinge of surprise at this
smart summary of her private business, together
with a twinge of uneasiness as she remembered
the Hall letter. Kirkby must be reminded about
it, she thought, the moment he came in. . . . But
she forgot it again instantly as she began a recital
of her plans, her hot face growing hotter, and
her hands moving restlessly. The future became
more and more real to her as she talked, just as
it had been made more real by the mere moving
of the furniture. She found herself telling Dolly
not only about the measuring and the packing,
but about the conditions and people awaiting
her over the water. She was not always quite
certain whether what she was relating existed in
point of fact or only in last night's dream, but
it did not matter. Such discrepancies as there
might be counted for nothing in the main im-
mensity of her statement.

Dolly made the most satisfying listener that
anybody could desire, her own hands twitching
and her own eyes shining. 'It's like a fairy-story,
I'm sure!' she declared, when at last the other,
short of further facts for the time being, was
beginning to repeat herself. 'I've heard a deal
about Canada, one way and another. My cousin,
Jessie Bowness married, this last year, and went
out to the same part as your Ellen.'

'Oh, ay?' Mattie replied indifferently, getting
somewhat heavily to her feet. 'Help me shove

this cupboard back again where it come from,
there's a good lass.'

'She lives near Ellen an' all,' Dolly went on,
setting her sturdy little shoulder to the cupboard.
'She's moved there just lately. She doesn't see
much of her, she says, as they're both so throng,
but she sends me news of her every now and then.'

Mattie said, 'Oh, ay?' again, as some answer
seemed to be needed, but every letter of the little
phrase bristled defensively. She had the same
impression of interference as at the sight of
Ellen's packet, the same sensitive fear of being
twisted from her path. . . . 'Lend me a hand with
this table now,' she continued quickly, hoping
that Dolly's cousin Jessie might drop out of the
conversation.

But Dolly had no intention of parting with
such an adjunct until it had yielded its utmost to
the interest of the occasion. She was too much
absorbed by her own prospects to be greatly
aware of another person's reactions, as well as
too highly excited to refrain from talking. Moreover, she thought in all innocence that Mrs.
Kirkby would be only too glad to listen to anything that she could tell her about Canada. Her
cousin Jessie, therefore, was so much present
with them during the afternoon, that it seemed
to Mattie sometimes she had only to turn herself
about in order to see her.

'Jessie isn't best suited with Canada,' Dolly
said, when the table had been restored to its
place, and the articles which usually reposed
upon it had returned to grace it. 'She says it's
so different.'

'Different to what?' Mattie enquired, affecting

obtuseness from a growing sense of annoyance.
'I don't rightly follow.'

'Different to England, she means, and the
things she's been used to, over here. She says
there's times she feels she might as well be in
the moon, it's all so strange.'

'Well, and why shouldn't it be?' Mattie returned, slapping down a book with unnecessary
vehemence, and then discovering it to be Kirkby's mother's Bible. 'It's like to be different,
isn't it, seeing it started a deal later?'

'Ay, I told her that, when she was complain-
ing about folks being scattered about like, except
when you got to the big cities. But Jessie was
always the sort that liked a crowd, even if it
meant sitting on other folks' knees or sleeping
three in a bed. . . . But it isn't only that,' she
continued, when she and Mattie between them
had removed the packing-case from the larder.
'There's the climate as well. She says it's that
cold in the winter you could get yourself frozen
stiff before you'd know anything about it.'

'I reckon *I'd* know all right, anyhow,' Mattie
retorted grimly, although not without an inward
qualm. Her particular brand of rheumatism,
acquired by a lifetime spent in damp gardens,
was peculiarly, if incongruously, susceptible to
frost. 'Ay, and if I was getting melted, either,
come to that!'

'Then there's the houses,' Dolly said, her
plump hands busy all the time clearing and
straightening. 'You should just hear her about
the houses! Them sort, you know, made of bits
of wood, as you build yourself? Hen-hulls, Jessie
says they are,—hen-hulls and nothing else!'

The elder woman felt a cold wrath take possession of her as she heard the precious house of her dream described in this derogatory manner. If Dolly's cousin Jessie had indeed been present at that moment, it would doubtless have gone hard with her. As she was not, Mattie was forced to content herself with glaring across the kitchen at Dolly, who, however, was busy putting a drawer in the dresser to rights, and could not see her.

'No place to swing a cat, Jessie says, and that ugly an' all! She says she'd give the eyes out of her head for a nice bit of mortared stone. "Something like that grand cottage of Mrs. Kirkby's," she says, "up at the gardens at the Hall." I once brought her up here on a message or something, if you remember, and she was that taken with this spot there was no holding her.'

Mattie did not remember, as it happened, and was, at that moment, as far as it was possible to be from wishing to remember. Her exasperation at the onslaughts of Dolly's cousin Jessie was only to be measured by her growing sense of helplessness in face of them. She had, however, just discovered something to say that might possibly put her out of court for good and all, when Dolly, passing to another drawer, flowed steadily onward.

'As for the folks out there, she hasn't a good word to say for them, home or foreign! A lot of bounders, she says,—barring always your folks, you'll understand, Mrs. Kirkby. The shop-folk, Jessie says, are that impudent she can bare bring herself to speak to them. Talk to you like as if they'd known you all your life, and call you "my dear" as soon as look at you!'

'I'd like to hear anybody calling me "my dear" before I had asked 'em for it!' Mattie said furiously, fingering a tea-cup with such fierceness that she broke the handle. The retainers connected with a big house have always a curious sense of being a species apart, and in spite of her rebellion she was not exempt from it.

'Likely Jessie did ask for it,' Dolly said soothingly, though without turning to look at her. 'I always thought her a bit free. . . . But the things she says about the folks as belong are nothing to what she says about the folks out from England. They fair ruin the place, she says— barring always your belongings, Mrs. Kirkby, as I said before. They're that stuck up, she says, each of 'em trying to best the rest, that you'd fair bust out laughing if you didn't feel that mad at 'em. I reckon Jessie's done her bit of sticking up as well, and it didn't come off, and that's what makes her so wild.'

'I don't know why any of them should be stuck up, I'm sure,' Mattie burst out before she had time to think,—'folks as didn't make good over here, and thought another country'd likely do the job!'

'Why, that's what Jessie says, Mrs. Kirkby!' Dolly said, looking at her now, and with definite surprise. 'Leaving their country for their country's good, is how *she* puts it. But I didn't look to hear you saying the same, and with your folks doing so well an' all!'

'Some on 'em,' she continued, before Mattie could find breath to speak again, 'make out they were that swell at home you'd likely think as they'd have brought their coronets with them!

There's some Madisons, she says, from over
Witham way, as is that full of themselves they
can hardly walk. They tell folks they had a big
farm over here, with a pedigree herd of the best;
whereas everybody knows they had nothing but
a milk-round as was more like a water-round,
by a deal!'

But Mattie had had more than she could bear
for the time being of Jessie's depressing reflec-
tions. A fresh picture of Canada was forming
before her eyes, blotting out the fine-hued image
which she had made for her own enchantment.
Already its glamour was blurred beneath Jessie's
touch, as frost-traceries are blurred by the rub
of a rough finger. She was appalled, too, by her
sudden, contemptuous speech, with its astonishing infidelity to her past beliefs. She had always
thought of the Canadian adventurers by the
brave title of pioneers, and would have been
proud to have made one of their gallant company. It seemed the last treachery of all that
she should have nursed that subtle contempt, so
that in a moment of idle annoyance it might set
a sneer upon her lips.

With a brusque movement she put an end
both to Mrs. Machell's monologue and to her
final dealings with the dresser.

'Let's get at t' parlour now, if you don't mind,'
she said, bustling before her into the dismantled
room. She was now just as anxious to get the
house put back to rights as she had wanted,
earlier on, to pull it all to pieces. Subconsciously
she was thinking that, when the place was tidy
again, the trouble that was growing in her mind
might possibly smooth out, too. . . .

The two women had a pleasant hour together arranging the little-used furniture, over which they spent more time than was necessary out of sheer enjoyment. Mattie found Mrs. Machell an entranced auditor as she dwelt upon its merits, pointing out its beauty of shape or gloss or the elegance of its handles. Pictures and vases had their histories related at full length, succeeded by records of clocks and epics of antimacassars. Dolly fingered and valued, praised and exclaimed, wondering to herself all the time how many of the precious objects would come her way at the sale.

'I'll have a bad time, I doubt, before I've settled what we're to take!' Mattie laughed, handling her treasures more and more fondly under Dolly's appreciation. 'I thought I'd hardened my heart to part with some of them, this morning, but, now that I'm looking at 'em again, I'm not so sure! There's no sense, though, in taking a chair-leg more than we're obliged. It'll cost enough, as it is. I doubt, anyhow, I'll have to make up my mind to leave pictures and knick-knacks behind.'

Dolly's heart leaped as she looked at a pair of bright pink vases, trimmed with an excellent imitation of sugar icing, seeing them already as her very own.

'Photo-frames and such-like won't pay for the taking, either,' Mattie was saying hesitatingly, 'though wild horses 'emselves wouldn't make me part with the photos. I've a regular stack of 'em as They've sent me, year in and year out, especially of the children. Some folks'd say it was nonsense taking photos along when you're

going to see the folks themselves, but I've grown
that used to them I've got to have them.'

She remembered now that she had not yet
spent the hour with the grandchildren which she
had promised herself earlier, and proceeded to
take it, setting them forth to Dolly with that
sense of proud showmanship which the first
generation almost invariably seems to feel towards the third. It was impossible to believe,
listening to her vivid description of its looks and
ways, that she had never yet set eyes upon a
single member of it. Smiling and happy, she had
found for herself again that first ecstasy which
she had felt upon awakening from her dream.
Canada was again what she had thought it to
be, as she laughed and talked, wearing always
that inward look of those who ponder upon
hidden treasure.

'Luke's youngest, they say, is as like me as
a couple of peas, and Joe's second takes after
Kirkby. He's a bit darker, perhaps, and he's
brown eyes instead of blue, but there's no mis-
taking where he comes from, either in looks or
manners. Little Eric, they call him, after his
mother's father, though I don't know why they
need go out of the family when there's so many
good names shouting. I'm right set upon little
Eric. . . . Maggie's May frames something grand
at the piano, and Ellen's Sally shapes to have a
voice. . . . Luke's eldest's getting on for twelve,
and can manage a motor-mower . . . leastways,
they say he can, though I doubt they're putting
it on.'

'Jessie can't abide Canadian children,' Dolly
cut in, introducing that unpleasant person for

the first time into the parlour. 'Real nasty about 'em, she is. She couldn't abide English children, either, if it comes to that, judging from what parents and such-like used to say about her when she taught school. But Canadian children, she says, are that uppish and wild there's no doing anything with them. Like savages, you'd think they were, if you swallowed everything you heard from Jessie. Fine children to look at, she says, and healthy and all that; but that noisy and full of beans they fair make an English person tired.'

Mattie had a horrid vision of a narrow and crowded house, with Kirkby and herself hemmed in by leaping, shouting children. She herself had once rather rejoiced in noise, though Kirkby had always hated it; but she was not so sure now that, after all these years of silence, she would not hate it, too. Luke had two other boys besides young Joe of the motor-mower, as well as a little girl just over a year old. He was fond of company, too, and was never so happy as when extending hospitality. Also he had that piano, she remembered with dismay, upon which both relatives and friends came eagerly to practise. . . .

The homes of the younger children had nothing better to offer, for they, too, had growing families, and in even smaller houses. It was true that she and Kirkby would have their own home before so long, but she could not think of it now with her early happy passion. It seemed vulnerable to her now, and no longer a haven of contentment. For the first time in her life she saw the good stone walls of her English cottage as a frame for privacy and peace.

'Jessie says Canadian children *aren't* children as we know 'em,' Dolly was saying blandly. 'She says they grow up that fast it's hard to remember they've ever even been babies. They're grown folks, she says, before you can hardly turn round, same as that fine lad of Luke's you said could manage a motor. I reckon you'll be surprised, Mrs. Kirkby, by the time you get there, to find how they've all come on.'

Mattie turned to the door with the same sharp movement with which she had endeavoured to rid herself of Jessie in the kitchen. That last stroke of hers, dealt through Dolly's innocent tongue, had gone a great deal nearer home than she cared to realise. Like most grandmothers, she had thought of the children as children only, hardly believing that in the future they would be grown-up people. And especially she had thought of little Eric as remaining always little Eric. . . . Yet already, as she remembered, a year had passed since they had sent her his last picture. By the time she got out to him, she reflected grimly, he, too, might have risen to the dignity of the motor-mower!

'Time we were having tea,' she said firmly, waving Dolly before her through the door. 'You'll be wanting it, I'm sure. As for me, I'm that worn out with all that shoving and siding, I could do with a dozen teas instead of one!'

Back in the kitchen, however, she was diverted by still another matter, which kept the tea waiting a little longer. Going to a cupboard in the wall, she opened the door and stood looking at its contents.

'I can't make up my mind what to do about

my jam,' she said, as Dolly joined her. 'It fair
goes to my heart to leave it. Yet it seems silly,
doesn't it, to go hugging jam-pots and such-like
across the ocean? I doubt it'll have to be put
in the sale.'

'Folks' ll be fighting like cats for it, if it is!'
Dolly laughed, peering admiringly round her
shoulder. Even at this time of the year the
shelves were still half-filled with rows of glisten-
ing jars, making, with their white caps topping
their coloured bodies, a smart and polished regi-
ment. 'It's a long while back since I first heard
tell there was nothing to beat your jam.'

Mattie looked pleased, and her voice lost the
rather dull tone which had suddenly come into
it since her late depression in the parlour.

'Well, I've always prided myself on getting it
just so,' she said, eyeing the glories of the cupboard proudly. 'It's been my hobby, as you
might say. Getting the best of everything, that's
the secret,—the best fruit and the best sugar, and
making sure of the boiling. Not but what like
enough there's a knack to it as well, same as
there is for making butter and setting hens.'

She ran her hand fondly over the white paper
carpet above which the jams glowed like so many
jewels, the raspberries looking like pressed gar-
nets against the prison of their glass, and the red
currant and apple jellies gleaming like ruby and
yellow topaz.

'There's plenty to go at, yet, as you can see,
even though we're well past the turn of the year.
I always make a fairish amount, in case we get
a bad year after a good one. 'Tisn't as if my
jam wouldn't keep; in a good season, I reckon,

it'd keep till the Day of Judgment! . . . This
shelf 's near all rasps, and that 's apricot and a
bit of marrow. There 's some blackberry jelly
behind, and a taste of wine-berry. We haven't
a deal of gooseberry and rhubarb, but there 's a
lot of plum. That pot or two of black currant
is just for when Kirkby gets a cough; and here's
where I keep my Best Strawberry.'

The red had come into Dolly's face as she
looked, gloating over the housewife's riches with
honest pleasure. Catching her breath a little as
Mattie stopped, she broke into quick speech.

'Likely you'll know, Mrs. Kirkby, what we're
hoping 'll come to Len? Mr. Kirkby was right
kind when he spoke about it, this morning. It's
early days to be talking, perhaps, but I thought
you wouldn't mind. . . .'

Mattie took her hand away from the shining
pot which she was stroking as a man strokes the
glossy coat of a horse, and looked round slowly.
'Talking about what?' she enquired, looking at
the colour in Dolly's face, and then away again.

'About Len applying for head place, if Mr.
Kirkby gives up,' Dolly said, growing more and
more nervous with every second. 'I shouldn't
have said anything, perhaps, but I thought you'd
be sure to know.'

For quite a long time Mattie was silent from
sheer surprise, not so much at Dolly's announce-
ment as at her own reception of it. No more
than to Kirkby had it occurred to her to specu-
late as to his probable successor, but, if ever she
had arrived at speculation, she would have been
certain that it would not trouble her. Yet here
she was, filled with anger and scorn, not only

on Kirkby's account, but actually on her own! Len's reaching out for the gardens which she had always hated should have been nothing to her, by rights; yet the very suggestion had set her seething with injured pride and pain.

'Nay, I've heard nothing about it, not I,' she managed to get out presently, trying to keep out of her voice her conviction that Len was an impudent monkey and a robber. 'But he'll be as likely as anybody, I should say, if it comes to choosing.'

Dolly's face glowed at this grudging praise, and she went forward with fresh confidence.

'That's right good of you, Mrs. Kirkby, seeing it's your own business we're after. I shouldn't have mentioned it but for the jam. But I'd be glad, if you're selling, to takè some of it over before the sale——'

She stopped as Mattie put out her arms again towards the shelves in a gesture which she could not interpret, but which was, as a matter of fact, a gesture of protection. Now it was Dolly as well as Len who seemed a thief, stretching out greedy hands to her own most precious belongings. She saw her moving about her home, sitting in her chairs, walking in the cool of the evening in her sacred garden. Her heart rose against her in a rage of distress which almost threatened to choke her. At that moment she could have driven the other woman from the house with blows. . . .

With agitated movements she began to push the jars as far back on their shelves as they would go, thrusting them out of sight and danger like a hen protecting her chickens. She closed the door with a bang, and snapped the lock with a click; and then, normal again with the shutting away of the threatened treasure, turned to Dolly, smiling.

'Ay, well, we'll talk about that later, when we've got things settled. Now I'm wanting my tea. Fill kettle and boil it, will you, while I set the cloth? . . . We're taking this over seriously,' she added, with a laugh, 'and forgetting it's just pretence!'

Dolly laughed, too, not only in polite recognition of the assumption with which they had started out, but because she felt relieved. There had been a strong feeling of tension in the air as they stood before the cupboard, and she was glad to get away from it. For the first time it crossed her kindly, unthinking little mind that things might have been better conducted, that afternoon. . . .

But she was soon at her ease again when they were seated at their meal; pleasantly conscious, as they kept telling each other, laughing, how well they had earned it. Her confidence returned, which had so nearly been shattered by the episode of the jam, and she let herself babble freely. Mattie found herself listening with interest to local gossip, and giving fervent attention to the local scandals. Hitherto, she had never cared a rap what happened in the hamlet, and could only conclude that this was one of the many changes which had come upon her to-day.

She had sworn to herself that she would not mention Canada again, but before they were half-way through the meal she had broken her intention. By the time she had poured the

second cups of tea she was gone abroad, taking
an interested Dolly with her. Seated at a cottage tea-table, they were yet gold-seekers and
explorers, game-hunters in the Rockies, and adventurers shooting the rapids. Their lungs were
braced by the air of the Strong Country, and
its distances lightened their eyes. The wind that
blows over the prairies filled and freshened the
little room.

'I'd a dream about it, last night,' Mattie said
presently, reverting to that solemn and lovely
subject a little shyly. 'I was There, just as I'm
here now, and with none of that nasty crossing.
I saw the places and the folks and the insides of
the houses. . . . And everything was as nice as
could be, in spite of your cousin Jessie!'

With her own lips she had invoked the demon
of the situation, and instantly it was at grips with
her. Dolly, dashed by the sense of insecurity
which had alarmed her before tea, had kept a
guard on her tongue as soon as Canada was
mentioned. But now Mattie, of her own accord,
had raised that guard, and she rushed in briskly.

'Jessie wouldn't know a nice spot if it up and
told her about it,' she said gaily. 'She was always
a wet blanket. . . . But they'll get the surprise of
their lives when they hear you're coming, Mrs.
Kirkby. Jessie says they've all of 'em given up
hopes of it long ago.'

A sudden quiet seemed to fall and envelop
Mattie, a quiet which spread and spread and
travelled over the kitchen. After a long moment
—'Who told her they'd given up hope?' she
enquired, stilly.

'Ellen told her herself,' Mrs. Machell replied,

uneasily conscious that the tension was return-
ing. ' "Father'll be getting past it, is what she
says, and I reckon so will Mother." She's a
grand plan now for coming over to you instead.
She's just breaking her heart, Jessie says, to get
back again over here. . . . She talks of bringing
little Sally with her when she comes, and leaving
her, if you want her. She'll be a help to you,
she says, now you're beginning to get on; and
Sally's as keen as mustard to come and live with
Granny.'

She stopped then, startled by the loudness of
her voice in the growing stillness, which seemed
at the same time both to accentuate it and re-
buke it. Looking across at her hostess, she felt
almost panic-stricken at the change which had
come upon her. It was impossible, she said to
herself, that those few chattered words should
so greatly have disturbed her. As if it mattered
what Jessie said, or what she chose to repeat!
Yet Mattie was sunk in her chair as if the vigour
which usually sustained her had suddenly de-
parted from her. Exhaustion had drained the
blood from her face, and without its customary
bright colour it looked somehow smaller. And
wrapping her round about was that curious cur-
tain of quiet; a shroud, as it were, automatically
produced for something that had ceased to
be. . . .

Glancing at the clock, Dolly stood up sharply,
setting the china ringing.

'I'll have to be going, Mrs. Kirkby,' she said
as quietly as she could, yet shrinking again from
her voice as it smote upon the silence. 'Len 'll
be wanting his tea. I'll just have time to lend

you a hand with the washing-up, and then I must be off.'

She had still another moment of panic before Mattie stirred, afterwards getting to her feet in a series of rather helpless movements. Dolly watched her with troubled eyes, wondering always how far she was responsible for the sudden situation. Even now that Mattie was standing up and moving about, she felt ill at ease with her. The absurd thought flashed through her mind that the Mrs. Kirkby who had got up was not the same Mrs. Kirkby who had sat down! . . .

Between them, they got the washing-up put through in record time, which yet seemed unnaturally long because of the heavy silence in which they did it. Mattie's work was as efficient as ever, but it seemed to have lost its spring. Her hands, moving with dull sureness among the cups and saucers, looked strangely old and weak. Dolly was dull, too, her brain groping its way back over the talk of the afternoon, and anathematising both her own foolishness and the grumblings of Cousin Jessie. It was with a sense of acute relief that at last she put on her hat and hurried to the door.

'Well, I'll be saying good day to you, Mrs. Kirkby,' she announced hastily to the still only half-recognisable figure of Mattie which had followed her. 'It's been real pleasant to have a chat. If you want a bit of help again when it really comes to packing, you've only to let me know.'

Mattie spoke to her then, though in an altered tone which corresponded to her altered presence. With an obvious effort she made her little speech of thanks,—Dolly moving restlessly the while,—and then bade her wait a moment. Going back into the kitchen, she reappeared with a pot of her Best Strawberry.

'Nay, I want you to take it,' she insisted, firmly if dully, as Mrs. Machell protested. 'You've been right kind. I'll give you them pink vases, if you'll have 'em, before the sale, but anyhow I'd like you to have a taste of my good strawberry.'

The tears came into Dolly's eyes. Regardless of the jam-pot, she put her arms round Mattie's neck and hugged her.

'I don't need presents just for enjoying myself!' she said, laughing and crying together. 'Eh, Mrs. Kirkby, but I'd be right glad if I heard as you weren't going!'

She was gone herself then, running across the gardens, jam-pot in hand, and Mattie waited until she had lost sight of her. Her lips had quivered a little at the warm pressure of Dolly's cheek, but they did not quiver now. Her figure straightened itself slightly as she turned on her heel, and went back slowly, but with set purpose, into the darkening house.

VI

SHE went back into the kitchen and sat down at the table from which the tea-things had been removed, and which now wore its evening glory of crimson cloth. The sight of the cloth reminded her that Kirkby had not yet come in for his meal, and she wondered what had become of him. But she forgot him again in the urge for settlement with herself which had suddenly seized her. Sinking herself in the problems which beset her, she lost all consciousness of time and place.

She sat heavily in her chair, with the heaviness of exhaustion, but with less of that air of lowered vitality which had frightened Mrs. Machell. A little force had returned to her joined hands, laid loosely along the table. Her face, lifted and looking straight before her, was the face of one who at the same time sits in judgment and awaits the decision of some tribunal.

She was still numb from the shock of Dolly's communication, but she was bracing herself all the time. She was trying to make herself understand that she had still to decide about Canada, still to set the balance dipping one way or the other. She had thought the choice made long since, clinched long ago beyond all possible change. But the truth was that you could neither test nor be tested by a situation which had not as yet arisen. She saw now that the decision had never really been made at all; that it never could have been made until Kirkby had written the letter. . . .

She had forgotten, too, that, while she waited, time had been at work, busily adding its make-weights on this side or on that. She had forgotten that people alter . . . that places alter . . . that she herself, even in the strict mould of her obsession, might possibly alter. . . . Behind her set face she was filled with fear that some still-unnoticed change might tip the scale against her.

So many ages seemed to have fled since the joy of the morning that she peered back at it with dim eyes as at some memory of childhood. Yet the steps by which she had come to this pass had been so swift that her brain swam at their mere remembrance. But they had only seemed swift because of the suddenness with which revelation after revelation had been sprung up-on her. The truths lying behind those changes of thought and scene must have been growing in secret for many a long year.

It was not only the whinings of Cousin Jessie which had taken her courage from her, stealing it, hour by hour, as if it was her very life-blood that they drained. The dream itself had under-mined it, puzzling and depressing her even while it glorified and exalted. She remembered the Questions, and shrank from the finger of warning which they so obviously had pointed. And she remembered that Ellen . . . but she was still too bruised and shocked to dare to dwell upon Ellen.

And after the dream there had been other por-tents and signs; each of them, as it were, putting out an unseen arm in order to stay her. All day long she had been called to attention by the things about her, as well as by the sudden, un-wished-for rising of old memories. Both within and without, as it were, she had been attacked, and before each attack had retreated a step further. All day long it had been brought home to her that she was exchanging the substance for the shadow, and that, in her insistence upon Canada, she was cutting herself off from the things which really mattered.

She said to herself angrily, as if accusing some outside power, that she had not known that places and houses could hold you against your will. She had tried to keep herself free, like a soldier awaiting his orders, and she had never once been free. Not only that, but it was she herself who had been forced to betray herself. Even while she was nursing and keeping warm her hatred of her surroundings, her heart was beginning to love them. Even while she had imagined herself to be facing steadily forward, she was already beginning to look back.

Dick Nelson had been right in saying that, no matter how you might fight against it, you were bound to settle, in the end. She had been angry about it, at the time, angry and contemptuous, but she saw what he meant, now. The gardens had grown no wider for her as time went on, but they had grown deeper. She had taken root. . . . It seemed as if the place where you had suffered held you as surely in the end as the place where you had been content. . . .

And in the same way people got hold of you, after a while . . . even those you disliked, let alone people like Mrs. Grisedale and Mrs. Ellwood. In spite of yourself they became part of your life,—that life which you had not wanted, perhaps, which had either been thrust upon you, or which you had chosen by mistake, but which nevertheless you had steadily gone on living. You could not keep yourself away from people, no matter how you tried. Even if you shared nothing else with them, you shared the same countryside. Your life was marked by the milestones of their happenings, just as their lives were marked by yours. And, when the time came to die, you lay down together to sleep in the same soil. . . .

She was too old for Canada, she said to herself, accepting the fact calmly because as yet it had not come home to her. Not too old in body, perhaps, in spite of her age, but almost certainly in spirit. You could not fret and fight, year after year, as she had fretted and fought, without something wearing out in you. And even her body felt too old to-night for the land of which she had always thought as a place of vivid youth. She would feel better in the morning, of course, —better and more equal to things,—because you always did feel better in the morning. It was one of the lessons of life that you could face things in the morning which you could not face at night. But always the night came again. . . . In any case, something told her that to-day she had touched what was for her the highest point of living. After to-day she would begin definitely to grow old.

Safety was what you needed most when you were beginning to get on; not to be high adventurers and pioneers. Pioneers and adventurers weren't safe,—couldn't be, in the nature of things. Whatever happened, she and Kirkby would have certain dangers to face, even though they were not going actually into the wilds. Dangers from people and food, from climate and travel and strain. . . . There were dangers everywhere, of course,—even here; but long custom had taught them how to avoid them. You got used to most of your dangers, except for those unforeseen; and when you were used to your dangers they were no longer very dangerous.

Safety and peace and quiet, and a certain amount of ease; not hen-hulls and yelling children, such as Cousin Jessie had pictured. Jessie, of course, had been drawing the long bow, even if she had not been telling absolute untruths. But it would be different from England, nevertheless. Whatever Luke's home might be like, it would not have the settled dignity of the home in which he had been reared. As for their own, which had yet to be built, it would have even less than Luke's. It would have no dignity, because it would have no memories and no past. It would be empty, and they would not have time to fill it. They would barely have grown used to it, and it to them, before death, with a crooked finger, would beckon them both out.

It was too late, she said to herself again, and felt through her calm the upstriking pang which the words inevitably evoke. It was true, as Dick said, that you could wait too long, so that, when the time came, and the chance offered, you were not able to take it. And the reason you were not able was because you had nothing left with which to meet it. The strength which you needed for new conditions had been squandered long ago; frittered away, day by day, in striving and rebellion.

The children thought it too late, too. . . . Her heart contracted as she remembered that, and she drew in her breath sharply. They had ceased to look for her long since,—if it was true what Jessie had told Dolly. It seemed a betrayal beyond pardon that they should not have gone on hoping as long as they could; at all events until she, who had lived on that hope, had finally resigned it. But she had never hinted at such a thing, not even in the latest of her letters. Perhaps they had laughed at the letters, she thought, shrinking; had mocked, even if ever so kindly, at the old mother who would not own herself defeated. . . .

At least they had not mocked her when they wrote, nor had they ever implied that they had ceased to expect her. They had kept it up, just as she had kept it up, and with all the old happy anticipation. And for long enough now it had been just pretence . . . that is, if you could believe Jessie. She felt suddenly that she hated letters and the things that they could do. . . . Jessie's letters, which had brought about this present trouble . . . the letters from the children, without which she might possibly have settled down long since. . . .

She came at last to the thought of Ellen, and forced herself to meet it. It was Ellen who had hurt her most,—Ellen, who had been nearest to her, and had always understood her. Not only had she ceased to believe that she would come, but, with the plan for her own visit growing in her mind, she must also have ceased to hope for it. She had told a complete stranger that she was breaking her heart, longingly looking back to the home she had left so gladly. She had not told her mother that she was breaking her heart. . . . Mattie felt the desolation of one who, dedicated to some cause, finds that the comrade with whom he has travelled has secretly turned back.

She remembered Ellen's packet now, and, getting up to look for it, returned with it resolutely to the table. She opened it slowly, fumbling with paper and string, and without any interest in what she was doing. Her mind, persistently turned inward upon its sorrow, refused to focus for more than a second upon any external object. All that she could think of at the moment was the hard fact of Ellen's backsliding, and the breaking of the bond which had so long existed between them.

There was a photograph in the packet, as she had thought, and presently she had unwrapped it and had it lying before her. There was no accompanying letter that she could find; but there was nothing in that, as she had had one, only yesterday. Taking the picture in her hands, she made a determined effort to fix her attention upon it.

After that first glance at it, however, she made as if to throw it down, for the woman in it was not Ellen. This was a middle-aged stranger, with traces of hard work in her face and hands, a little droop to her head and a slight stoop to her shoulders. The lips smiled, it was true, but behind the attempt at gaiety the face was tired. Even the clothes she wore had something a little strange about them to Mattie's English eyes.

Yet for all that it was still Ellen. . . . Even as she looked she saw the likeness stand out; first, in the curve of the cheek, and then in the curve of the mouth. They were Ellen's eyes, when she came to study them, though the laughing and dancing in them had sunk deeper. They were Ellen's hands, too, which, even to this day, had kept their old childish habit of clutching at her gown.

Her heart swelled as she looked, both on her own account and on her daughter's, thinking of the light, laughing thing that had gone out of the cottage, to return to her in this guise. She had known that she would look older, of course, and, as far as she could, had taught herself to expect it. But she could never have believed that the years would make so much difference. She remembered that Ellen was younger than Dolly,— Dolly, with her plump, straight, little figure and cheerful, unlined face,—and felt the tears that were in her heart rise up and fill her throat.

A horror of Canada seized her,—horror and fear of the land which had played such havoc with Ellen, and which had taken her away from her in more senses than she knew. For it was neither the added years nor the look of endurance which troubled her, after the first. People grew older in England, as well as anywhere else, and Ellen had never been very strong. . . . What frightened her was the unmistakable air of another country, turning her daughter into a stranger.

She sat for a long time trying to will the young Ellen back into the picture, and saw the youth come into it by degrees as the spring green comes upon the hedgerows. And presently, when she had her again, the longing to see her grew

greater than she could bear. Silently and un-
known to her, as she stared, the tears ran down
her face. . . .

She must see her, at all costs, she said to herself, in spite of Ellen's lack of confidence and the
bitterness of betrayal. It would be harder to go
now, both because of her own clearer vision of
things, and because of the fading impulse from
Over There which had done so much to sustain
her. The glamour had gone out of the enterprise
for ever. But she could not afford to wait until
Ellen should find both money and opportunity
for her visit. At all costs, she must go to Canada.

But, even as she made her decision, she remembered the sea, and shrank from it in her
mind as if from an actual presence. It had
frightened her, even in her morning freshness;
in her evening weariness it became a stalking
horror. Her passion for size and space, together
with her power of visualisation, turned upon her
now to her own undoing. The Atlantic rose up
against her in its sullen depth and strength, in
chain upon chain of endless, rolling mountains.
Presently, as it seemed, the advancing terror was
in the garden and in the house, and under the
waves of her huge vision she saw herself sink and
drown. . . .

She came back at last to find herself twisted
in her chair, with her eyes fixed upon some half-
seen but definitely soothing object. As her mind
cleared she found that she was looking through
the open larder door, and out through the window beyond, which vignetted the privet hedge.
She could see the lawn, too, shadowy and
mysterious with the evening, and the rose-bush,

slimmed and thinned to almost elfin proportions.
Over the hedge-top there still lingered a segment
of silvered, tranquil sky. . . .

Her heart stopped pounding as she looked,
and the choking terror which had sprung on her
out of the ocean slowly loosed its grip. The peace
of the garden reached her even in the house,
making an exquisite stillness where the sea had
roared and rolled. She sat drinking in the quiet,
watching the sky fade and the lawn dim as veil
after veil was laid upon them. . . . And then
again she remembered Ellen.

She would never be able to get to Ellen if she
could not face the sea, and she knew now that
she could not face it. There was no deliverance,
after all. All that she could do was to sit and
wait for Ellen to come, and Ellen might never
come. . . . She sprang to her feet, crying aloud
that she was trapped, as Kirkby, down in the
garden, was crying that he was trapped. She
could neither go nor stay, she said to herself, get
to Ellen nor remain here. Life, after all these
years of bitterness and despair, could do nothing
better for her than to get her into this trap. . . .

With the supreme terror upon her of those
who see themselves caught by life, she ran to the
door, and beheld the bowed figure of Kirkby,
dusky and ghost-like in the distance. Leaving
the house, as if it was her own self that she left,
she went running and stumbling towards him
across the gardens.

PART III
THEIRS

H E came hurriedly to meet her, forgetting himself and his personal misery in this sudden alarm. 'What's to do, Mattie? What's wrong?' he enquired anxiously, as they drew near to each other in the shadows.

She stumbled the last few yards, and clung to his arm. He could feel her shaking. Even in the dusk he could see the marks of tears upon her face.

'What's to do?' he said again.

She made an effort to control herself then, and heard her voice come out as if from some other person.

'We can't go,' she said, and her voice broke. 'It's no use! We can't go.'

He felt, as it were, a sudden lightening of the atmosphere about them; as if the sun, already gone some time, had for the moment broken out afresh. . . . But he was too tired to feel more; too tired, certainly, to feel glad. Indeed, he was conscious, rather, of a faint resentment that the problem which had cost so much to settle should be about to be re-opened.

'Best come into the house, hadn't you?' he said, evading it for the moment, and gently urging her back again in the direction from which she had come. 'It's getting damp, out here.'

She nodded her head with a docility which sat strangely upon her, and, still holding to his arm, allowed him to lead her back. She said nothing more as they went, only catching at her breath from time to time with little signals of distress which awoke in him a succession of answering quivers. The gardens saw them enter the house together, and disappear into the further gloom of the kitchen.

The sight of the red tablecloth aroused her temporarily, as it had done before. 'Eh, now! You've never had your tea,' she sighed, shocked out of her preoccupation by that great forgetfulness.

'I'll get a bite of something presently,' Kirkby said, taking off his hat with the limp gesture of a man whose weariness had long since passed the stage of desire for food and drink. 'It's you I'm bothered about. What's been to do you've gone and got yourself in such a state?'

She dropped back into the seat from which she had raised herself in order to go to him, and sank her head on her hand.

'It's just that,' she said. 'We can't go. . . . I've seen it coming on like, all day, and now it's come to bide.'

He eyed her thoughtfully, not daring to take what she said literally,—scarcely, indeed, wishing at that moment to take it literally. . . . 'You're over-tired, that's what it is,' he said, at last. 'You haven't hurt yourself, have you, pulling that furniture about?'

'Nay, I've taken no harm.'

'Likely you haven't thought on to get your own tea, neither?' he enquired.

'Ay, but I have,—and a rare good tea an' all!' She winced at the remembrance, recalling the happy half-hour that she and Dolly had spent before Cousin Jessie had struck her to the heart. . . . 'But we can't go.'

He stood hesitating in front of her, his mind wholly occupied by the need to get her comforted. She was tired, he said to himself, and folks didn't always mean what they said when they were tired. His heart ached as he looked at her, remembering as he did the fine joyfulness of spirit with which she had parted from him at noon.

'You'd best tell me about it, hadn't you, Mattie?' he ventured presently. 'You'd feel a deal better if you could tell somebody.'

'There's nothing to tell. . . .' She avoided his eyes, feeling the colour rise in her cheek. She was ashamed that even Kirkby should see her in this moment of defeat. 'Nothing much, I mean,' she went on, in a dull tone, 'and what there is you'd likely not understand.'

'I could try, anyway, Mattie.'

She gave a deep sigh and put her hands before her face. He waited patiently, standing with that still poise of his in which he seemed to breathe as quietly as a flower. And almost at once she began to speak, jerkily at first, but gradually gathering smoothness and speed, and keeping her hands always on either side of her face as if they guarded her.

'It's just we've waited too long. . . . Things alter if you wait. You stop wanting things you've always wanted, and you get to like things you used to hate. And you get old, waiting. I didn't know till to-day I was getting old.'

'You're not old, Mattie.'

'I'm old inside,—old in my heart. Folks as keep their hearts up never get old, but I've not kept mine. If I could have kept my heart up,

I'd have been young, even at a hundred, but I've not kept it up. I've been letting go, all the time, though I didn't know it.'

'How d'you mean—letting go?'

'Giving up about going to Canada,—that's what I'm trying to say. I've been thinking all these years I'd be mad to go when the time came. I thought I'd be that glad I wouldn't mind what I found Over There or what I'd to leave behind. And it isn't like that at all. Now it's really come to it, I'm—afraid.'

'How d'you mean—afraid?'

She gave a little laugh that was more dreary than any sob,—the laugh of the naturally brave person who for the first time in life comes under the domination of fear.

'Afraid of near everything, it seems to me! . . . Afraid I'll get hankering after things, this side, when it's too late to come back. Afraid of breaking my heart Over There, as I've broken it over here. . . . Afraid of all the new folks and new sights. Afraid of the sea——'

She shuddered as she said the last word, seeing, even as she spoke, the first wave of her vision come rolling back upon her. Kirkby looked surprised.

'What's put that into your head?' he asked, puzzled. 'You've never let on before you minded the sea?'

'I've always minded it,' Mattie said. 'First time I set eyes on it,—ay, and long before that. But I wouldn't let on about it even to myself. I made out it wouldn't matter, just as I made out other things wouldn't matter. But I was only cheating myself all the time. They *do* matter, and I do mind; and now I'm old I haven't the courage to face 'em.'

'You'll face 'em right enough to-morrow,—see if you won't! You're over-tired, to-night. I'll be bound you weren't bothering about the sea when you woke, this morning!'

He spoke purposely in a light, bantering tone, hoping to stir her out of her trouble; but she shook her head.

'There'll be another night to-morrow. . . . It's the nights you've got to think of, when you're getting old. And it isn't only the sea. There's other things as well.'

'Tell me the other things, Mattie.'

She shook her head again, but almost at once she was launched upon her tale, as if the little movement had flung her into the tideway. As well as she could she described to him her reactions during the day, beginning with the little cloud which had shadowed even the dream itself, and which had grown to such proportions by the evening. Her talk halted and turned upon itself and wandered to and fro, until not only the tale but the hours themselves seemed twisted into a tangle. Something, however, of the actual state of things emerged finally from the muddle, together with a fairly definite indication of how it had come about.

She told him, still shielded by her hands, how the house and the garden had caught at her unawares, rising up against her with armed memories which she had not known to possess the power to wound her. She told him of Dick's grumbled warnings, of her passion for the privet hedge, of the jealousy and injured pride with which she had found herself facing Mrs. Machell. She told him at great length of the underminings of Cousin Jessie. And, at the last, sighing and half-sobbing, she told him of the betrayal of the children, and the greater treachery of Ellen.

'That's what's getting at me most,' she finished, hating her own voice as she heard it quiver. 'That's what's done me down. T'other things was bad enough, of course, fretting me right and left till I was near frantic. But I'd have got over 'em, likely, after a bit, and when I was feeling better. Likely I would, that is. I'm not so sure. . . . But what beats me is the children going back on us and thinking we wouldn't come. Folks as stop believing in a thing like as not stop wanting it,—that's how it seems to me.'

Kirkby had stood silent during the first part of the recital, and had seated himself silently when he found it promised to be a long one. Once, later, he got up to look for the lamp, only to find that Mattie had forgotten to fill it. This oversight on the part of one usually so methodical and efficient told him more than even the hurried and broken talk with which she was assailing him. Lighting a candle which he discovered on the mantelpiece, he sat down again, setting the light between them.

He was not thinking much as he listened; only allowing her to pour her story into his mind, so that, when the time came, and she was silent again, he might find the right words with which to cheer her. Still less was he feeling. . . . He had already exhausted his own powers of emotion; first, in that journey into the past which

he had taken, across the river, and then in his
final revolt and recession in the garden. He felt
utterly detached from the situation which was
riving Mattie in twain as if it was with an actual
devil that she strove. Whether they went or
stayed made no difference to him at the moment.
He had passed, for the time being, to a plane
where the things of this world could no longer
affect him, either for good or evil.

'It's Ellen bothers me most,' Mattie was saying, the quiver in her voice becoming more and
more pronounced. 'I'd have thought Ellen
would have looked for me till I was in my coffin,
—ay, and after that! Jessie says she talks nowadays of coming here instead, but I doubt she
never will. Likely she'll wait and wait and never
come, same as I've waited and waited and never
gone. . . . And if she puts it off a deal longer
I won't answer for it we'll know her. That's her
photo she's sent, over there, and for more than
a while I made sure it was somebody else.'

Kirkby turned his eyes towards the photograph on the table, and turned them away again.
He had no desire to look at it just then, or to
test the truth of what Mattie was saying. His
power to interest himself in such things would
return to-morrow, when he would welcome even
a doubtful presentment of his absent daughter.
But to-night he had passed beyond his children,
and felt no bond with them. They were no more
to him at the moment than the transplanted
sapling is to the parent stem from which it was
once grown.

'You're taking a deal for granted, it seems to
me,' he said, at last. 'You've only Len's wife's

word for it about Ellen and the rest, and not at first hand, neither. Yon cousin of hers needs taking with a deal of salt.'

Mattie nodded drearily.

'You're right, there! She's one of them do-nowts as has always a sight to complain of, wherever they are. . . . But I feel it's true, all the same. It's only natural folks should give up looking for you when you've been so long on the road.'

'I don't see it matters whether they've given up or not. They'd be just as glad to see you, once you'd got across.'

'It *would* matter,' Mattie said. 'Something 'd have gone . . . broken . . . nay, I can't explain!' She stopped, hunting vainly for words with which to convey to him that the motive power would be crippled, the circuit hopelessly snapped. . . . 'But it wouldn't be the same.'

He gazed at her with his clear, faded eyes, wondering to himself how far it was wise to attempt to argue with her.

'You'll not take kindly to stopping, Mattie,' he said presently, tentatively but bravely. 'You've got to remember that.'

'I'm not likely to forget it.'

'It isn't as if you wouldn't feel different in the morning, you know. You're tired, to-night. You'll get hankering again, I doubt, as soon as you're rested.'

'I doubt I will.'

'Folks don't change that easy,' Kirkby persisted. 'You've been set on Canada so long, you'll find it hard to put away from you.'

'I've got to try.'

'There'll be letters coming an' all——' he continued firmly, and she put out her hand, crying, 'Nay, now! Don't, don't!' but he steeled himself against her. However it hurt, they had both of them got to be sure that she knew what she was doing.

'And there's the grandchildren, you'll think on; you've not forgotten them? You'll likely never set eyes on them if you don't go. It costs a deal to go back and forwards, these days, and there's time as well. Sally'll likely come, if Ellen's bringing her to stop, but not Joe's lad or the rest——'

She stumbled to her feet, throwing out her hand a second time as if to lay it across his patient, insistent mouth.

'Nay, now! *Don't*, I tell you! D'you think I don't know what it'll be like, and how it's going to hurt before I've finished with it? Day and night I'll remember,—day and night. But it's got to be borne. Some way or other I've got into a trap, and I doubt I'll never get out.'

'You *can* get out, Mattie,' Kirkby said gently. 'You've only to say the word.'

'Nay, but I can't.' She looked down at her hands as she rested them on the table, as if already she saw ghostly fetters forming about her wrists. . . . 'Words won't make any difference, nor letters, neither. It's my own self makes the trap,—being too old, and being afraid of things. You should have let us go when I was younger and able to face it. You've kept us here too long.'

''Twasn't me, Mattie,' Kirkby said, wincing a little for the first time. ''Twas just life.'

'Nay, it was you, all right!' she said, lifting her head again. She sent him a look which he had seen more than once before, a hard, sneering look that called him an enemy and hated him as it said it. He met it quietly. . . . 'It was you kept us. And now I've got to go eating my heart out till I die!'

Moving away from the table, she began to walk up and down the room, clasping and unclasping her hands.

'And it'll be worse now than it was before,— a deal worse, a deal harder to bear. There'll be nothing to hope for, now. . . . It'll be just prison again, and the same old life right on to the end. If I'd known things were going to turn out like this, I'd have finished myself long ago!'

She was crying now and wringing her hands, stumbling blindly from point to point, and blundering against things in her passage. From time to time she looked wildly from side to side, as if she saw the cottage-walls closing in upon her. From his seat by the table Kirkby sat and watched her, as only the night before he had watched the firelight beat against the ceiling. . . .

She came suddenly to a pause, and, putting out a clenched fist, struck it against the mantel-piece.

'I can't bear it!' she said in a loud tone. 'I can't bear it, and I won't! There's my children waiting for me Over There, and I'll get to them, if I have to walk. It's my life that I ought to have had, and that I've been cheated out of, and I mean to have it.' Her voice rose higher. 'What is it goes wrong with things when folks get cheated out of their lives?'

Her tone lowered itself then as suddenly as it had risen, and became passionate and pleading. 'I take back everything I said just now,' she told him gently. 'I want to go. . . .' Turning unsteadily, she came to him, holding out her hands. 'You'll not think any more about what I said? You'll let us go?'

'We'll go, Mattie. Don't you fret.'

'It'll be just as it was, this morning?' she pursued, unsatisfied. 'The same as it was, last night?'

'Just as it was, Mattie.'

A smile touched for a moment her tear-wet face, and for the first time he felt the tears spring to his own eyes. She looked at him kindly.

'You mustn't be wild with me for chopping and changing like this. I can't help it. I've got to see 'em all again, and the grandchildren and the houses. I've *got* to see them. You can't plan and work for a thing all your life, and not get it in the end. It'd kill you, if you didn't get it,— leastways, it would me. . . . But I shan't chop and change again. I'll get the letter written first thing in the morning, and the one for the passage as well. We must begin thinking about the sale, too, as soon as may be. I did a lot of planning, this afternoon, along with Mrs. Machell. I don't know that I'm best pleased to think of her living in this house, though *she*'s pleased enough, to be sure! I near told her to think on it was my home and not hers, and would she kindly re-member it? There was the jam an' all,—I'd nigh forgotten the jam. . . .' Her voice wavered as she spoke, and she looked away from him. 'And the privet hedge,—I don't know how I'll abide her having the privet hedge. . . . Len, too, swaggering about the spot, and thinking he's as good a man as you. . . . I reckon they're thinking already we're as good as overseas——'

She stopped then, and into her eyes came the fixed stare of one who regards a great and imminent danger. The cry which came out of her throat was no longer the cry of one beating against walls, but the cry of one who drowns. . . .

'Nay, but we can't! We can't! I'm cheating myself again. Just cheating myself, that's all. . . . I'll never get to Canada, not this side o' the Judgment!'

Flinging herself heavily into her seat, she laid her head on her arms, and her great sobs shook the silence. Outside in the darkness a little wind got up, sighed along the paths and was gone again into the darkness. An owl called, flapping with clumsy wings across the square of the window, and went out towards the river. A sweet breath came in from the gardens, where there were no flowers as yet to scent them.

Kirkby sat where he was for a long time, with his gaze fixed upon his wife's bowed head and labouring shoulders. It was the only way, as he knew, to put a real end to the business, to exorcise, by those cruel tears, the demon of her forty years' obsession. Canada went out of her as she wept, and all the beautiful hope which for so long it had represented. Through every pore of her, as it were, ran out the poison of her misery and discontent. She would be broken, perhaps, when she came to herself, but she would no longer be tormented. She would be older, perhaps,—perhaps permanently grown old,—but she might also have found the things which belonged truly to her peace. . . .

Yet, even in the restraint of his measured wisdom, he could not refrain from making some attempt to comfort her. From time to time he put out an apparently unnoticed hand, and drew it back again. Presently, when he could bear the situation no longer, he got up and stood beside her.

He said: 'Don't cry, Mattie! . . . Mattie, don't cry,' smoothing her roughened hair and patting her shoulder and cheek. She paid no attention, as far as he could gather, until presently the sobs quietened and the shaking lessened. And instantly, as if at some signal for which he had patiently waited, he began to speak.

'I just want to say again, Mattie, that we'll go if you really want. Likely you'd rather leave it over until the morning, but I doubt it wouldn't be wise. I couldn't go through this sort of thing very often, nor you, neither. We'd be best to fix it to-night. . . . And you don't need telling that, if you could make up your mind to it, I'd a deal rather not go. I've had as bad a day thinking about it all as I ever remember.' His detachment broke a little, and pain crept into his voice. 'I've loved the place, and I doubt I can't leave it.'

'I've hated it, and I can't leave it!' Mattie sobbed, lifting her head a moment and letting it drop again.

'There's some sorts of hate as is very near love,' Kirkby said absently, without hearing what he was saying. 'Only just now, you said that to-day you'd seen it different.'

Mattie sobbed again, remembering the enraptured hours in which that miracle had happened, and realising that, now that she was a prisoner once more, the enchantment would have passed for ever.

'It was just because I was going to get away from it,' she wept; 'that's all. To-morrow it'll all be nasty, just as before.'

'It'll never be just as nasty, Mattie, whatever you think,' Kirkby said firmly. 'Once you've looked at a thing with love, you never rightly forget it. It comes creeping back into your heart, no matter how often you turn it out.'

She said nothing to that, and presently he went on again, speaking in a dreamy tone as if he were weaving a spell of some sort about her, and as if the sentences were being dropped by something outside him into his tired brain.

'We've not done so badly together, Mattie, you and me, when you come to think of it. We've quarrelled a deal about this Canadian business, I know that, but we've not done so badly, all told. We've had a good life together in a beautiful place, which is more than a lot of folks get. We've been God-fearing folk, on the whole, and we've as good children as ever stepped. We've had a good life, Mattie, and we've been together a long while. Children matter a sight, I know, but we matter to each other more. We've made something between us in this spot as we'll never have anywhere else. We've made our lives. . . . When folks get to the end of things, all that they've got left to them is just their lives. . . .'

She had ceased crying long before he stopped, only sighing and bowing her head upon her hand as she had done at the beginning. Her mind, utterly wearied and over-strained, had for compensation that curious quality peculiar to extreme exhaustion of seeing clear in flashes. By virtue of those flashes, so much more vivid and poignant than those of the normal course of thought, she was able for the first time to see life as Kirkby saw it. For the first time she saw the dignity and the beauty of the life to which he clung, and to which such characters as his own owed their inward essence. Canada had gone out of her, as he had hoped, and into the great space which it had left flowed Kirkby and his gardens.

She remembered now that he had not been in the dream, and felt again the sudden shoot of fear with which she had first realised it. The violence of that pang showed her what she had never known until now, that Kirkby was more to her than the children. He had not been more to her once, as she had to admit. In her vigorous youth and middle-age she had found him tiresome, with his gentle ways and lack of push. But the years had done their work. . . . They had grown nearer together as time went on, while the children had grown further. They had been through things together of which neither the children nor anyone else could ever have any knowledge. Their very quarrels had brought them together, as if in fighting each other they had merely been fighting in order to get to each other. Now, in this last struggle of all, the last veil had been cleared away, and they saw each other close. . . .

Kirkby was right when he said that all that

you had at the end of your life was just your life. This was their life, which they had made together in this place, a completeness and a dearness, now that they came to look back upon it, formed, not only out of their happy hours, but out of their grim ones. It was theirs, and theirs only, shared by nobody else in the world; a thing so much their own that it seemed as if even God Himself must refrain from looking at it. . . . It was this life, which was all that they had, that Kirkby had feared to lose, if they went away. . . .

She drew her hand across her eyes, and, taking a deep breath, pulled herself into an upright position.

'Well, that's over,' she said bravely enough, though her voice shook. 'Over for good. . . . You needn't fear I'll ever bother you about Canada again.'

'You'll feel better to-morrow,' Kirkby said, falling back, after his flight of eloquence, on that eternal and feeble consolation; and she laughed a little, though without rancour and without bitterness.

'Better—or worse! . . . Ay, well. Never mind about that. It's over, as I said. . . . It seems queer to me now, though, always being so sure that I should go.'

Her mind went back to the dream, with all its richness and reality, and in one of those strange flashes she saw both its meaning and its hidden comfort. She had always known that some day she would go to Canada, and she *had* gone, although not in the body. Nor would her body ever be able to go now, because she herself would prevent it. But the dream had shown her a way by which her spirit, at least, could sometimes gain release. One of these days, if life pressed too hardly upon her, she might be permitted to go again.

She took up, after that, the encouraging thought of Ellen's coming, and the short but beautiful happiness that her visit offered. For already she was fast recovering her natural poise. Her mind, clearing and gaining in strength, fastened upon hope after hope, as a child, strange to its feet, fastens and clutches for support. Already she saw Ellen in the house, and, after Ellen, the little girl; and she rose up out of her desolation and grasped bravely at the future.

Kirkby was asking for the Hall letter when she heard him again; that letter upon which so short a time ago the whole of her salvation had hung, and which now seemed as remote and immaterial as if it had never existed. They hunted for it together, and discovered it at last in a spot where they could have come across it only by the merest accident. She could not remember putting it there, nor had she seen it handled by Mrs. Machell. It was almost as if some inner self of her own had secretly put it away, knowing long before she knew it herself that she would have no use for it.

Going to the hearth, where the fire, though low, was still red and smouldering, Kirkby made as if to tear the letter across.

'I'd best burn it, hadn't I?' he paused first to ask her, looking at her. 'It's better not left about.'

For one last moment a pang shot through her

as she stood there, staring at it, seeing the chance which she had forgone made concrete and passing from her for ever. She put out her hand as if meaning to snatch it from him, and then dropped it again. 'Nay, burn it,' she said, turning away, and quivered at the tearing of the paper. Even turned away she saw the little flame which the letter made before it died down and was no more. . . .

'I'll see about getting you a bite,' she said then, moving away from the hearth, and remembering with a housewife's shame that Kirkby must be nearly starving. Candle in hand, she went to and fro between kitchen and larder, and soon had the belated meal set and waiting on the table. When it was ready, she called to him where he stood at the house-door, staring into the darkness.

'I've just remembered I've promised my pink vases to Mrs. Machell!' she laughed ruefully; her voice, in spite of all that she had been through, sounding natural and brisk. 'That's if I went to Canada, I mean; and, now that Len won't be getting the job, I don't like to disappoint her.'

'I'll buy you another pair, if you want 'em,' Kirkby answered, without turning. 'Mason and Mawson's in Witham is as full of them as it can stick.'

Mattie laughed again, with cheerful disgust.

'Nay, then, I've no use for 'em, if there's that many going begging! . . . Your supper's ready for you now, if you feel like having it.'

He made no movement, however, to come within, and after a moment she went across to her jam-cupboard and threw it open. For several

minutes she stood gazing soberly at its contents,
while Kirkby, staring into the dark, saw his
dawnbell rising blue and exquisite against the
soil. . . .

She fastened the cupboard again presently,
and turned about with a little shiver.

'Best shut the door, hadn't you?' she called to
Kirkby. 'It's getting a bit chilly.'

He shut it.

PRINTED IN
GREAT BRITAIN
AT THE
UNIVERSITY PRESS
OXFORD
BY
JOHN JOHNSON
PRINTER
TO THE
UNIVERSITY

A LIST OF THE

WORLD'S
CLASSICS

Oxford University Press

THE WORLD'S CLASSICS

A SERIES in constant progress, containing over four hundred volumes, and offering in a size adapted for the pocket, and at a low price, the most famous works in the English language, with more than a few translations. Many of the volumes contain introductions by the best modern writers.

POCKET SIZE, 6 × 3¾ inches (as this list). Large type, on thin opaque paper, in superfine art cloth.

A NUMBER of the volumes are also obtainable in Pebble grain Moroccoette; also in Sultan-red Leather or Natural grain Morocco. These are specially recommended for presentation.

THE VOLUMES are obtainable only through the booksellers.

IN THE FOLLOWING LIST the books are classified as below:

Anthologies
Autobiography
Biography
Classics—Greek and Roman
Drama
Essays and Belles Lettres
Fiction (Short Stories are grouped separately)
History
Letters
Literary Criticism
Philosophy and Science
Poetry
Politics, Political Theory, and Political Economy
Religion
Short Stories
Travel and Topography

AN INDEX OF AUTHORS is given at the end of the list.

LATEST ADDITIONS

¶ *Drama*

FIVE PRE-SHAKESPEAREAN COMEDIES: EARLY TUDOR (Fulgens and Lucrece, The Four PP., Ralph Roister Doister, Gammer Gurton's Needle, The Supposes). Edited by *F. S. Boas* (418).

FIVE ELIZABETHAN COMEDIES (Friar Bacon and Friar Bungay, The Old Wives Tale, Campaspe, The Shoemaker's Holiday, The Merry Devil of Edmonton). Edited by *A. K. McIlwraith* (422).

¶ *Essays, &c.*

ENGLISH CRITICAL ESSAYS. (Twentieth Century.) Selected and edited by *Phyllis M. Jones* (405).

MODERN ENGLISH ESSAYS. Selected by *H. S. Milford*. Second Series (406).

READING AT RANDOM: A 'World's Classics' Anthology (410).

TOLSTOY. On Life, and Essays on Religion. Translated, with an Introduction, by *Aylmer Maude* (426).

¶ *Fiction*

AUSTEN (JANE). Northanger Abbey. Introduction by *Michael Sadleir* (355). Persuasion. Introduction by *Forrest Reid* (356). Sense and Sensibility. Introduction by *Lord David Cecil* (389).

FRENCH SHORT STORIES. Selected and translated by *K. Rebillon Lambley* (396).

GERMAN SHORT STORIES. Translated by *E. N. Bennett*, with an Introduction by *E. K. Bennett* (415).

HOLME (CONSTANCE). Crump Folk going Home (419). The Lonely Plough (390). The Old Road from Spain (400). The Splendid Fairing (416). The Things which Belong— (425). The Trumpet in the Dust (409).

RABELAIS. Gargantua and Pantagruel. Translated by *Urquhart* and *Motteux*, with notes. 3 vols. (411–13).

SCOTT. Short Stories. With an Introduction by *Lord David Cecil* (414).

TOLSTOY. Nine Stories (1855–63) (420). War and Peace. A revised translation by *Louise* and *Aylmer Maude*, embodying Tolstoy's final amendments. 3 vols. (233–5).

TROLLOPE. Orley Farm. 2 vols. (423, 424). *In preparation.*

¶ *Poetry*

A BOOK OF SCOTTISH VERSE. Compiled by *R. L. Mackie* (417).

¶ *Politics, &c.*

SPEECHES AND DOCUMENTS ON THE BRITISH DOMINIONS (1918–1931), from Self-Government to National Sovereignty. Selected, with an Introduction, by *A. Berriedale Keith* (403).

COMPLETE LIST OF THE SERIES

¶ *Anthologies*

A BOOK OF NARRATIVE VERSE. Compiled by *V. H. Collins.* Introduction by *Edmund Blunden* (350).

A BOOK OF SCOTTISH VERSE. Compiled by *R. L. Mackie* (417).

AMERICAN CRITICISM. Representative Literary Essays. Chosen by *Norman Foerster* (354).

ENGLISH ESSAYS, chosen and arranged by *W. Peacock* (32).

ENGLISH ESSAYS, 1600–1900, chosen by *S. V. Makower* and *B. H. Blackwell* (172).

ENGLISH ESSAYS, MODERN. Two Series. Selected by *H. S. Milford* (280, 406).

ENGLISH PROSE from MANDEVILLE to RUSKIN, chosen and arranged by *W. Peacock* (45).

ENGLISH PROSE, chosen and arranged by *W. Peacock* in 5 volumes: I, WYCLIFFE to CLARENDON; II, MILTON to GRAY; III, WALPOLE to LAMB; IV, LANDOR to HOLMES; V, MRS. GASKELL to HENRY JAMES (219–23).

ENGLISH PROSE, Narrative, Descriptive, Dramatic (MALORY to STEVENSON), compiled by *H. A. Treble* (204).

ENGLISH SONGS AND BALLADS, compiled by *T. W. H. Crosland.* New edition, with the text revised, and additional poems (13).

ENGLISH SHORT STORIES (Nineteenth and Twentieth Centuries), selected by *H. S. Milford.* Three Series (193, 228, 315).

ENGLISH VERSE. Edited by *W. Peacock.* Vol. I, Early Lyrics to SHAKESPEARE (308). Vol. II, CAMPION to the Ballads (309). Vol. III, DRYDEN to WORDSWORTH (310). Vol. IV, SCOTT to ELIZABETH BROWNING (311). Vol. V, LONGFELLOW to RUPERT BROOKE (312).

LETTERS WRITTEN IN WAR-TIME (Fifteenth to Nineteenth Centuries), selected and arranged by *H. Wragg* (202).

A MISCELLANY OF TRACTS AND PAMPHLETS. Sixteenth to Nineteenth Centuries. Edited by *A. C. Ward* (304).

PALGRAVE'S GOLDEN TREASURY, with 190 pages of additional poems by *FitzGerald, Tennyson,* the *Brownings, Arnold,* &c. (133).

READING AT RANDOM. A 'World's Classics' Anthology (410).

¶ *Autobiography*

AKSAKOFF (SERGHEI). Trans. by *J. D. Duff.* A Russian Gentleman (241). Years of Childhood (242). A Russian Schoolboy (261).

CELLINI (BENVENUTO) (300).

DE QUINCEY (THOMAS). Confessions of an Opium-Eater (23).

FRANKLIN (BENJAMIN). The Autobiography, edited from his original manuscript by *John Bigelow* (250).

GIBBON (EDWARD). Autobiography. Intro. *J. B. Bury* (139).

HAYDON (BENJAMIN ROBERT). The Autobiography. Introduction and Epilogue by *Edmund Blunden* (314).

HOLCROFT (THOMAS). Memoirs, continued by *W. Hazlitt* (302).

HUNT (LEIGH). Autobiography. Intro. *Edmund Blunden* (329).

MILL (JOHN STUART). Autobiography. Introduction by *Harold J. Laski* (262).

MORITZ (C. P.). Anton Reiser. Intro. *P. E. Matheson* (299).

TOLSTOY. A Confession, and What I believe. Translated by *Aylmer Maude* (229).

TRELAWNY (E. J.). Adventures of a Younger Son. Introduction by *Ethel Colburn Mayne* (289).

TROLLOPE (ANTHONY). Autobiography. Introduction by *Michael Sadleir* (239).

¶ *Biography*

CARLYLE. The Life of John Sterling. Introduction by *W. Hale White* (' Mark Rutherford ') (144).

CRABBE, LIFE OF. By his Son. Intro. *E. M. Forster* (404).

DOBSON (AUSTIN). Four Frenchwomen: Charlotte Corday, Madame Roland, Princess de Lamballe, Madame de Genlis (248).

EMERSON. Representative Men. (With *English Traits*) (30).

FRANCIS OF ASSISI (ST.). The Little Flowers ; and The Life of Brother Giles. Translated into English verse by *James Rhoades* (265).

GASKELL (MRS.). The Life of Charlotte Brontë (214).

HOUGHTON (LORD). Life of Keats (364).

JOHNSON (SAMUEL). Lives of the Poets. 2 vols. (83, 84).

MAUDE (AYLMER). Life of Tolstoy. 2 vols. (383, 384).

SCOTT (SIR WALTER). Lives of the Novelists. Introduction by *Austin Dobson* (94).

SMITH (J. T.). Nollekens and his Times. With Introduction by *Walter Sichel* (322).

TREVELYAN (SIR G. O.). Life of Macaulay. With a new Introduction by *G. M. Trevelyan*. 2 vols. (401, 402).

WALTON (IZAAK). Lives of Donne, Wotton, Hooker, Herbert, Sanderson. Introduction by *George Saintsbury* (303).

¶ *The ' Classics ', Greek and Roman*

AESCHYLUS. The Seven Plays. Translated into English Verse by *Lewis Campbell* (117).

ARISTOPHANES. The Acharnians, Knights, Birds, and Frogs. Translated by *J. Hookham Frere*. Intro. *W. W. Merry* (134).

HOMER. Translated by *Pope*. Iliad (18). Odyssey (36).

SOPHOCLES. The Seven Plays. Translated into English Verse by *Lewis Campbell* (116).

VIRGIL. The Aeneid, Georgics, and Eclogues. Translated by *John Dryden* (37).

—— The Aeneid, Georgics, and Eclogues. Translated by *James Rhoades* (227).

¶ *Drama*

BROWNING (ROBERT). Poems and Plays, 1833-42 (58).

CONGREVE (WILLIAM). Complete Works. 2 vols. Introduction by *Bonamy Dobrée.* Vol. I, The Comedies. Vol. II, The Mourning Bride, with Letters, Poems, and Miscellanies (276, 277).

EIGHTEENTH CENTURY COMEDY. FARQUHAR'S Beaux' Stratagem, STEELE'S Conscious Lovers, GAY'S Beggar's Opera, FIELDING'S Tom Thumb, GOLDSMITH'S She Stoops to Conquer (292).

EIGHTEENTH CENTURY, LESSER COMEDIES OF THE. Edited by *Allardyce Nicoll.* The five comedies are ARTHUR MURPHY'S The Way to keep him, GEORGE COLMAN'S The Jealous Wife, MRS. INCHBALD'S Everyone has his Fault, THOMAS MORTON'S Speed the Plough, and FREDERICK REYNOLDS'S The Dramatist (321).

FIVE PRE-SHAKESPEAREAN COMEDIES. Edited by *F. S. Boas.* Contains MEDWALL'S Fulgens and Lucrece, HEYWOOD'S The Four PP., UDALL'S Ralph Roister Doister, the anonymous Gammer Gurton's Needle, and GASCOIGNE'S Supposes (418).

FIVE ELIZABETHAN COMEDIES. Edited by *A. K. McIlwraith.* Contains GREENE'S Friar Bacon and Friar Bungay, PEELE'S The Old Wives Tale, LYLY'S Campaspe, DEKKER'S Shoemaker's Holiday, and the anonymous Merry Devil of Edmonton (422).

MARLOWE'S Dr. Faustus (with GOETHE'S Faust, Part I, trans. *J. Anster*). Introduction by *Sir A. W. Ward* (135).

RESTORATION TRAGEDIES. DRYDEN'S All for Love, OTWAY'S Venice Preserved, SOUTHERNE'S Oronooko, ROWE'S Fair Penitent, and ADDISON'S Cato. Introduction by *Bonamy Dobrée* (313).

SHAKESPEARE. Plays and Poems. Preface by *A. C. Swinburne.* Introductions by *Edward Dowden.* 9 vols. Comedies. 3 vols. (100, 101, 102). Histories and Poems. 3 vols. (103, 104, 105). Tragedies. 3 vols. (106, 107, 108).

SHAKESPEARE, Six Plays by Contemporaries of. DEKKER, The Shoemaker's Holiday; WEBSTER, The White Devil; BEAUMONT and FLETCHER, The Knight of the Burning Pestle, and Philaster; WEBSTER, The Duchess of Malfi; MASSINGER, A New Way to pay Old Debts. Edited by *C. B. Wheeler* (199).

SHERIDAN. Plays. Introduction by *Joseph Knight* (79).

TOLSTOY. The Plays. Complete edition, including the posthumous plays. Translated by *Louise* and *Aylmer Maude* (243).

¶ *Essays and Belles Lettres*

BACON. The Essays, Civil and Moral (24).

BROWN (DR. JOHN). Horae Subsecivae (Rab and His Friends, &c.). Introduction by *Austin Dobson* (118).

CARLYLE. On Heroes and Hero-Worship (62). Past and Present. Introduction by *G. K. Chesterton* (153). Sartor Resartus (19).

SMOLLETT. Travels through France and Italy (90).
STERNE (LAURENCE). A Sentimental Journey. Introduction by *Virginia Woolf* (333).
STEVENSON (R.L.). Virginibus Puerisque, & Across the Plains (296).
THACKERAY. The Book of Snobs, &c. (50).
THOREAU. Walden. Introduction by *Theodore Watts-Dunton* (68).
TOLSTOY. Translated by *A. Maude*. Essays and Letters (46). 'What is Art?' and Essays on Art (331).
TRACTS AND PAMPHLETS, from JOHN KNOX to H. G. WELLS (304).
WHITE (GILBERT). The Natural History of Selborne (22).
WHITMAN. Specimen Days in America (371).

¶ *Fiction* (For SHORT STORIES see separate heading)

AINSWORTH (W. HARRISON). The Tower of London (162).
AUSTEN (JANE). Emma (129). Pride and Prejudice (335). Mansfield Park (345). Northanger Abbey (355). Persuasion (356). Sense and Sensibility (389).
BETHAM-EDWARDS (M.). The Lord of the Harvest (194).
BLACKMORE (R.D.). Lorna Doone. Intro. *Sir Herbert Warren* (171).
BORROW (GEORGE). Lavengro (66). The Romany Rye (73).
BRONTË (ANNE). Agnes Grey (141). Tenant of Wildfell Hall (67).
BRONTË (CHARLOTTE). Jane Eyre (1). Shirley (14). Villette (47). The Professor, and the Poems of the Brontës (78).
BRONTË (EMILY). Wuthering Heights (10).
BUNYAN. The Pilgrim's Progress (12). Mr. Badman (338).
CERVANTES. Don Quixote. 2 volumes (130, 131).
COBBOLD (REV. RICHARD). Margaret Catchpole (119).
COLLINS (WILKIE). The Moonstone. Introduction by *T. S. Eliot* (316). The Woman in White (226).
COOPER (J. FENIMORE). The Last of the Mohicans (163).
DEFOE. Captain Singleton (82). Robinson Crusoe. Part I (17).
DICKENS. Barnaby Rudge (286). Christmas Books (307). Edwin Drood (263). Great Expectations (128). Hard Times (264). Old Curiosity Shop (270). Oliver Twist (8). Pickwick Papers. 2 volumes (120, 121). Tale of Two Cities (38).
DISRAELI (BENJAMIN). Coningsby (381). Sybil (291).
ELIOT (GEORGE). Adam Bede (63). Felix Holt (179). The Mill on the Floss (31). Romola (178). Scenes of Clerical Life (155). Silas Marner, &c. (80).
FIELDING. Jonathan Wild (382). Joseph Andrews (334).
GALT (JOHN). The Entail. Introduction by *John Ayscough* (177).
GASKELL (MRS.). Cousin Phillis, and Other Tales, &c. (168). Cranford, The Cage at Cranford, and The Moorland Cottage (110). Lizzie Leigh, The Grey Woman, and Other Tales, &c. (175). Mary Barton (86). North and South (154). Right at Last, and Other Tales, &c. (203). Round the Sofa (190). Ruth (88). Sylvia's Lovers (156). Wives and Daughters (157).
GISSING. Veranilda (349). Will Warburton (348).

¶ History

BARROW (SIR JOHN). The Mutiny of the *Bounty* (195).
BUCKLE. The History of Civilization. 3 volumes (41, 48, 53).
CARLYLE. The French Revolution. Introduction by *C. R. L. Fletcher*. 2 volumes (125, 126).
FROUDE (J. A.). Short Studies on Great Subjects. Series I (269).
GIBBON. Decline and Fall of the Roman Empire. With Maps. 7 volumes (35, 44, 51, 55, 64, 69, 74).
IRVING (WASHINGTON). Conquest of Granada (150).
MACAULAY. History of England. 5 vols. (366–70).
MOTLEY. Rise of the Dutch Republic. 3 volumes (96, 97, 98).
PRESCOTT (W. H.). The Conquest of Mexico. 2 vols. (197, 198).

¶ Letters

BURKE. Letters. Selected, with Introduction, by *H. J. Laski* (237).
CHESTERFIELD. Letters. Selected, with an Introduction, by *Phyllis M. Jones* (347).
CONGREVE. Letters, in Volume II. See under *Drama* (277).
COWPER. Letters. Selected, with Intro., by *E. V. Lucas* (138).
DUFFERIN (LORD). Letters from High Latitudes. Illustrated (158).
ENGLISH LETTERS. Fifteenth to Nineteenth Centuries (192).
GRAY (THOMAS). Letters. Selected by *John Beresford* (283).
JOHNSON (SAMUEL). Letters. Selected, with Introduction, by *R. W. Chapman* (282).
LETTERS WRITTEN IN WAR-TIME. Fifteenth to Nineteenth Centuries. Selected and arranged by *H. Wragg* (202).
SOUTHEY. Selected Letters (169).
TOLSTOY. Essays and Letters. Trans. by *L.* and *A. Maude* (46).
WHITE (GILBERT). The Natural History of Selborne (22).

¶ Literary Criticism

AMERICAN CRITICISM. Representative Literary Essays. Chosen by *Norman Foerster* (354).
COLERIDGE (S. T.) Lectures on Shakespeare (363).
ENGLISH CRITICAL ESSAYS. Selected and edited by *Edmund D. Jones*. 2 volumes. I, Sixteenth to Eighteenth Centuries. II, Nineteenth Century (240, 206).
HAZLITT (WILLIAM). Characters of Shakespeare's Plays. Introduction by *Sir A. T. Quiller-Couch* (205). Lectures on the English Comic Writers. Introduction by *R. Brimley Johnson* (124). Lectures on the English Poets (255). The Spirit of the Age. (Essays on his contemporaries) (57).
HORNE (R. H.). A New Spirit of the Age (127).
JOHNSON (SAMUEL). Lives of the Poets. 2 volumes (83, 84).
SAINTE-BEUVE. Causeries du Lundi. (In English.) Two Series (372–3).
SHAKESPEARE CRITICISM. (HEMINGE and CONDELL to CARLYLE.) Selected and Introduced by *D. Nichol Smith* (212).

¶ *Philosophy and Science*

(For POLITICAL THEORY and RELIGION see separate headings)

AURELIUS (MARCUS). Thoughts. Translated by *John Jackson* (60).

BACON. The Advancement of Learning, and the New Atlantis: Introduction by *Professor Case* (93). Essays (24).

CARLYLE. Sartor Resartus (19).

DARWIN. The Origin of Species. With a new preface by *Major Leonard Darwin* (11). Voyage of a Naturalist (360).

REYNOLDS (SIR JOSHUA). Discourses, &c. Intro. *A. Dobson* (149).

TOLSTOY. What then must we do? Trans. by *A. Maude* (281).

WHITE (GILBERT). The Natural History of Selborne (22).

¶ *Poetry*

ARNOLD (MATTHEW). Poems, 1849–67 (85).

BARHAM (RICHARD). The Ingoldsby Legends (9).

BLAKE (WILLIAM). Selected Poems (324).

BRONTË SISTERS, THE. The Professor, by CHARLOTTE BRONTË, and Poems by CHARLOTTE, EMILY, and ANNE BRONTË (78).

BROWNING (ELIZABETH BARRETT). Poems. A Selection (176).

BROWNING (ROBERT). Poems and Plays, 1833–42 (58). Poems, 1842–64 (137).

BURNS (ROBERT). Poems (34). Complete and in large type.

BYRON. Poems. A Selection (180).

CHAUCER, The Works of. 3 volumes. Vol. I (42); Vol. II (56); Vol. III, containing the whole of the Canterbury Tales (76).

COLERIDGE. Poems. Introduction by *Sir A. T. Quiller-Couch* (99).

CONGREVE (WILLIAM). Complete works in 2 volumes. Introductions by *Bonamy Dobrée*. I, The Comedies. II, The Mourning Bride, Poems, Miscellanies and Letters (276, 277).

DANTE. Italian text and English verse-translation by *Melville B. Anderson*, on facing pages, with notes. 3 vols. (392–4). Translation only, with notes, in one volume (395).

DOBSON (AUSTIN). Selected Poems (249).

ENGLISH SONGS AND BALLADS. Compiled by *T. W. H. Crosland*. New edition, with revised text and additional poems, 1927 (13).

ENGLISH VERSE. Vols. I–V: Early Lyrics to SHAKESPEARE; CAMPION to the Ballads; DRYDEN to WORDSWORTH; SCOTT to E. B. BROWNING; LONGFELLOW to RUPERT BROOKE. Edited by *William Peacock* (308–312).

FRANCIS OF ASSISI (ST.). The Little Flowers of St. Francis. Translated into English Verse by *James Rhoades* (265).

GOETHE. Faust, Parts I and II. Translated by *Bayard Taylor*. Intro. by *Marshall Montgomery* and notes by *Douglas Yates* (380).

GOLDEN TREASURY, THE. With additional Poems (133).

GOLDSMITH. Poems. Introduction by *Austin Dobson* (123).

HERBERT (GEORGE). Poems. Introduction by *Arthur Waugh* (109).

HERRICK (ROBERT). Poems (16).

HOMER. Translated by *Pope*. Iliad (18). Odyssey (36).

HOOD. Poems. Introduction by *Walter Jerrold* (87).

KEATS. Poems (7).

KEBLE. The Christian Year (181).

LONGFELLOW. Evangeline, The Golden Legend, &c. (39). Hiawatha, Miles Standish, Tales of a Wayside Inn, &c. (174).

MACAULAY. Lays of Ancient Rome; Ivry; The Armada (27).

MARLOWE. Dr. Faustus (with GOETHE's Faust, Part I, trans. *J. Anster*). Introduction by *Sir A. W. Ward* (135).

MILTON. The English Poems (182).

MORRIS (WILLIAM). The Defence of Guenevere, Life and Death of Jason, and other Poems (183).

NARRATIVE VERSE, A BOOK OF. Compiled by *V. H. Collins*. With an Introduction by *Edmund Blunden* (350).

NEKRASSOV. Trans. by *Juliet Soskice*. Who can be happy and free in Russia? A Poem (213). Poems (340).

PALGRAVE. The Golden Treasury. With additional Poems (133).

ROSSETTI (CHRISTINA). Goblin Market, &c. (184).

SCOTT (SIR WALTER). Selected Poems (186).

SCOTTISH VERSE, A BOOK OF. Compiled by *R. L. Mackie* (417).

SHAKESPEARE. Plays and Poems. Preface by *A. C. Swinburne*. Introductions by *Edward Dowden*. 9 volumes. Comedies. 3 volumes (100, 101, 102). Histories and Poems. 3 volumes (103, 104, 105). Tragedies. 3 volumes (106, 107, 108).

SHELLEY. Poems. A Selection (187).

TENNYSON. Selected Poems. Intro. *Sir Herbert Warren* (3).

VIRGIL. The Aeneid, Georgics, and Eclogues. Translated by *Dryden* (37). Translated by *James Rhoades* (227).

WELLS (CHARLES). Joseph and his Brethren. A Dramatic Poem. Intro. *A. C. Swinburne*, and Note by *T. Watts-Dunton* (143).

WHITMAN. A Selection. Introduction by *E. de Sélincourt* (218).

WHITTIER. Poems: A Selection (188).

WORDSWORTH. Poems: A Selection (189).

¶ Politics, Political Economy, Political Theory

BAGEHOT (WALTER). The English Constitution. With an Introduction by the *Earl of Balfour* (330).

BUCKLE. The History of Civilization. 3 volumes (41, 48, 53).

BURKE (EDMUND). Letters. Selected, with an Introduction, by *Harold J. Laski* (237). Works. 6 volumes. Vol. I: A Vindication of Natural Society; The Sublime and Beautiful, &c. (71). II: The Present Discontents; and Speeches and Letters on America (81). III: Speeches on India, &c. (111). IV: Writings on France, 1790–1 (112). V: Writings on Ireland, &c. (113). VI: A Letter to a Noble Lord; and Letters on a Regicide Peace (114).

ENGLISH SPEECHES, from BURKE to GLADSTONE. Selected and edited by *E. R. Jones* (191).

MACHIAVELLI. The Prince (43).

MAINE (SIR HENRY). Ancient Law (362).

MILL (JOHN STUART). On Liberty, Representative Government, and the Subjection of Women (170).

MILTON (JOHN). Selected Prose. Intro. *Malcolm W. Wallace* (293).

RUSKIN. 'A Joy for Ever', and The Two Paths. Illustrated (147). Time and Tide, and The Crown of Wild Olive (146). Unto this Last, and Munera Pulveris (148).

SMITH (ADAM). The Wealth of Nations. 2 volumes (54, 59).

SPEECHES AND DOCUMENTS ON BRITISH COLONIAL POLICY (1763–1917). Ed. *A. B. Keith.* 2 volumes (215, 216).

SPEECHES AND DOCUMENTS ON THE BRITISH DOMINIONS, 1918–31. Selected, with Introduction, by *A. B. Keith* (403).

SPEECHES AND DOCUMENTS ON INDIAN POLICY (1756–1921). Edited, with Introduction, by *A. B. Keith* (231, 232).

SPEECHES ON BRITISH FOREIGN POLICY (1738–1914). Edited by *Edgar R. Jones, M.P.* (201).

TRACTS AND PAMPHLETS, A Miscellany of. Sixteenth to Nineteenth Centuries. Edited by *A. C. Ward* (304).

TOLSTOY. What then must we do? Translated, with an Introduction, by *Aylmer Maude* (281).

¶ Religion

THE OLD TESTAMENT. Revised Version. 4 vols. (385–8).

APOCRYPHA, THE, in the Revised Version (294).

THE FOUR GOSPELS, AND THE ACTS OF THE APOSTLES. Authorized Version (344).

THE NEW TESTAMENT. Revised Version (346).

À KEMPIS (THOMAS). Of the Imitation of Christ (49).

AURELIUS (MARCUS). Translated by *John Jackson* (60).

BUNYAN. The Pilgrim's Progress (12). Mr. Badman (338).

KORAN, THE. Translated by *E. H. Palmer*. Introduction by *Reynold A. Nicholson* (328).

TOLSTOY. Translated by *Aylmer Maude*. A Confession, and What I believe (229). On Life, and Essays on Religion (426).

¶ Short Stories

AFRICA, STORIES OF. Chosen by *E. C. Parnwell* (359).

AUSTRIAN SHORT STORIES. Selected and translated by *Marie Busch* (337).

CRIME AND DETECTION. Two Series (301, 351). Stories by H. C. BAILEY, ERNEST BRAMAH, G. K. CHESTERTON, SIR A. CONAN DOYLE, R. AUSTIN FREEMAN, W. W. JACOBS, EDEN PHILPOTTS, 'SAPPER', DOROTHY SAYERS, and others.

CZECH TALES, SELECTED. Translated by *Marie Busch* and *Otto Pick* (288). Nine stories, including two by the BROTHERS CAPEK.

DICKENS. Christmas Books (307).

ENGLISH SHORT STORIES. Three Series. Selected by *H. S. Milford*. Introduction by *Prof. Hugh Walker* in Vol. I (193, 228, 315).

FRENCH SHORT STORIES. Eighteenth to Twentieth Centuries. Selected and translated by *K. Rebillon Lambley* (396).

GASKELL (Mrs.). Introductions by *Clement Shorter*. Cousin Phillis, and Other Tales (168). Lizzie Leigh, The Grey Woman, and Other Tales, &c. (175). Right at Last, and Other Tales, &c. (203). Round the Sofa (190).

GERMAN SHORT STORIES. Translated by *E. N. Bennett*, with an Introduction by *E. K. Bennett* (415).

GHOSTS AND MARVELS and MORE GHOSTS AND MARVELS. Two Selections of Uncanny Tales made by *V. H. Collins*. Introduction by *Montague R. James* in Series I (284, 323).

HARTE (BRET). Short Stories (318).

HAWTHORNE (NATHANIEL). Tales (319).

IRVING (WASHINGTON). Tales (320).

PERSIAN (FROM THE). The Three Dervishes, and Other Stories. Translated from MSS. in the Bodleian by *Reuben Levy* (254).

POE (EDGAR ALLAN). Tales of Mystery and Imagination (21).

POLISH TALES BY MODERN AUTHORS. Translated by *Else C. M. Benecke* and *Marie Busch* (230).

RUSSIAN SHORT STORIES. Chosen and translated by *A. E. Chamot* (287).

SCOTT. Short Stories. With an Introduction by *Lord David Cecil* (414).

SHORT STORIES OF THE SOUTH SEAS. Selected by *E. C. Parnwell* (332).

SPANISH SHORT STORIES. Sixteenth Century. In contemporary translations, revised, with an Introduction, by *J. B. Trend* (326).

TOLSTOY. Nine Stories (1855–63) (420). Twenty-three Tales. Translated by *Louise* and *Aylmer Maude* (72).

TROLLOPE. Tales of all Countries (397).

¶ *Travel and Topography*

BORROW (GEORGE). The Bible in Spain (75). Wild Wales (224). Lavengro (66). Romany Rye (73).

DARWIN. Voyage of a Naturalist (360).

DUFFERIN (LORD). Letters from High Latitudes (158).

MELVILLE (HERMAN). Typee (294). Omoo (275).

MORIER (J. J.). Hajji Baba of Ispahan. Introduction by *C. W. Stewart*, and a Map (238).

SMOLLETT (TOBIAS). Travels through France and Italy in 1765. Introduction (lxii pages) by *Thomas Seccombe* (90).

STERNE (LAURENCE). A Sentimental Journey. With Introduction by *Virginia Woolf* (333).

INDEX OF AUTHORS, ETC.

Further Volumes are in preparation.

October 1934